Hope
IN LETTERS

MARIA ÁVILA

Palmetto Publishing Group, LLC
Charleston, SC

For more information regarding special discounts for bulk
purchases, please contact Palmetto Publishing Group at
Info@PalmettoPublishingGroup.com.

ISBN-13: 978-1-944313-11-1
ISBN-10: 1-944313-11-7

For my family.

THE SPARROW'S RAINBOW

"Color me a rainbow," said the Tree Sparrow to the sky.
"Gladly," responded he. "But first I must cry, cry, cry."
And the sky shook with sorrow, recorded its sadness
    with thunder.
It struck the earth in rage with lightning and scattered
    heavy grumbles.
The howling winds shook everything, as the sky released
    its wailing cry.
The small Tree Sparrow cowered and whimpered to-
    wards the sky,
"I asked for a rainbow. Why did you send me such tor-
    ture?"
"Because, dear friend, for a glimpse of beauty, there
    must first always be sorrow."

Indifference is love's silent killer.

LIANA

I t's in the middle of a freezing winter day, while I'm waiting for my husband to come home from work, that I see the mailman walking to my door. I've been sitting by this window watching the day go by, feeling sorry for myself, attempting to nurse my bruised heart with doses of positive words. It isn't working. Every positive word appears to have a string of negative words trailing closely behind, and no matter how hard I try, I can't outrun my thoughts.

Slowly I unfold myself from the couch and head to the door. Looking through the peephole I watch the mailman deliver a few envelopes, which I know are bills; hopefully none past due. Peter seems to be getting a little forgetful lately. The mailman whistles, his breath leaving his lips in happy puffs. I don't understand how anyone could be so happy on a day so cold.

With a half turn he starts walking back toward the street. Our neighbor's lively, white Pomeranian barks out a greeting and does a few laps around his feet. When I see him turn carefully into their yard, so as to not step on the dog, I open my door and retrieve the mail. I shiver violently when the cold air hits me and quickly close the door. While I wait for my temperature to stabilize, I count my breaths making sure that my lungs fill as much as possible; which is another form of therapy that isn't working. After what seems like forever, I am somewhat warmer and I head to the loveseat to check the mail.

As I assumed, there's the water bill, the electricity bill and a slew of credit card offers. Then I see a different kind of envelope. It is lilac, my favorite color, and it has my name and address on the front. The letters flow softly from one to the next making my name look exotic, sexy. I feel a tingling in my bones and a shudder in my soul. There isn't a return address on its corner, adding to the mystery. Who could have sent it, and why is my body reacting with excitement?

I look up at the grandfather clock that's ticking the day away and notice that it's still not time for my husband's return. I'm never quite sure what time he'll walk through the door. If they have a big project at work, he'll stay past five. In the past few weeks they must've picked up a huge project because he's been coming home closer to seven. With this in mind, I make supper quite early every day, except on the days I have to work late, and keep it in the oven on a low temperature so it will stay warm, awaiting his return.

I look back down at the envelope, feeling my heart flutter and then I glance out my window. For some odd reason, I still don't want to open it. I know anyone else would've torn open the flap as soon as they'd discovered it, but I have always been more disciplined when it comes to prolonging excitement. I want to wait until it bubbles up through me and I can no longer stand it; until I feel like anticipation is going to kill me; until my hands begin sweating with nervous delight.

I watch as the world outside accepts a blanket of snow to cover its bareness. The day is still and white. If I could concentrate on only that, I could find peace. But life is not about watching a day go by, it's about choices. Some I wish I didn't have to make.

I flip the envelope and start to run my finger under the flap, carefully so I won't tear it. I still don't have a clue as to who sent it, but I have a premonition that what I'm about to read will affect me. I'm simply not sure if it will be in a good or bad way.

The flurries outside my window pick up, as does the fluttering of my heart while I pull the paper out of the envelope. I unfold it and purposefully do not look to see who has signed it. As I said, I am incredibly disciplined.

Things are meant to be read from top to bottom, left to right, and that is what I do.

Dear Liana,

Please forgive me for not introducing myself. It is better this way. I have a story to tell and I must tell it to you, since you're a key player, even though you have been unaware of such an occurrence.

You see, one day as I was strolling downtown, minding my own business, I saw this beautiful woman walking toward me. She was about 5'2", or 5'3"; of thin build and with long, caramel cream wavy hair. Eyes: chocolate, lips: glossy pink. I thought to myself that I had to be seeing visions or that my mind was playing tricks on me because on that particular walk I had been thinking about what I would like to see in the woman I would ultimately give my heart to.

Then you happened beside me and a quick whisper of the wind caught the sleeve or your silky, navy blue dress and it grazed me. A current of electricity bolted through me! I turned, shocked and unbelieving that I could have such a reaction to someone completely unknown to me. I began wondering if you were real . . . and sure enough, there you still were, walking away, alive and very much real.

I followed you, a feat made easier by your leisurely pace, like a true stalker, for this I apologize, but I had to know more. I confess this to you, not to scare you, please don't think of me as some maniac, I only wanted to know about you: your name, your

4

life, your likes, your dislikes, your passions and your heart.

It took some time, but finally I learned that you work at the library, you love the color purple and that you are a married woman. This last bit of information prevents me from walking up to your doorstep and making my presence known.

I realize you may be asking yourself why I decided to write. The answer is simple. Your eyes were sad. I feel the need to try to make them happy, but I'm not exactly sure how.

Oh, but wait! There is one thing that I can give you in hopes that I might succeed. Words. My words are not empty. My words are yet but humble creatures. These words I give to you for storage in your heart and in your mind. Carry them with you, pull them out when you need to. Caress them, like the wind did to your dress that one day and gave you to me.

Stop reading, if you must, and close your eyes. Envision everything that makes you happy and allow me to take you there. If you need a walk in the rain, let me take that walk with you. If you need a cry alongside a riverbank, let me be your shoulder to cry on. If you need to make a wish upon a star, let me be the one that finds the star that will make your wish come true.

Forgive me again. I should not speak to you like this. A woman such as you is honest and true. That is why I will admire you from afar. Maybe one day I will have the chance to reveal myself to you, but now is not the time.

With love and respect,
Your Admirer

With a sigh and a trembling hand, I lower the letter. I wipe away the tears that fell quietly as I read. What is happening? I look at the envelope again. Yes, that is my name. Who has sent this letter, very-much-so, addressed to me? Who could proclaim to have these feelings to-wards me? I can't even awaken something like this in my husband. Not now. Not anymore. So who?

How different it had been when Peter and I first met. Young and naïve I was ready to settle down with the first man who professed his love for me. And I fell for him. Hard. I remember when he took me dancing, how he had held me in his full, strong arms; my body pressed to his as we moved to the music and I thought it was all terribly romantic. I had read many romance novels that described bodies like his and what they could do to a girl like me. I blushed, ashamed and thrilled with the mischievous ways of my thoughts; and when he asked why my cheeks were pink, I told him it was the heat. He thought I meant from the room.

The music stopped and he went in search of drinks. Laughter and conversation skipped through the air as I waited. I smiled because it felt good to be right there, right then with him. When he returned, he handed me a cup and his eyes held mine. I knew then that I was his. A lively jig came on and back to the dance floor we went. Cigarette smoke was heavy in the air, but I transformed it into clouds that we danced through. I was a fairy-tale weaver.

We had met a few months prior. I, the typical bored store clerk waiting for my Prince Charming to rescue me from behind my register. He, the handsome gentleman who happened to walk in at the right time and embodied my description of a dashing prince. I wanted to find my true love, my happily ever after and yes, maybe even my rags-to-riches story. Although I wasn't dead set on that last one.

That day I was wearing a white dress, with a black belt that accentuated my tiny waist, my heels were three inches high and my hair was hairsprayed stiff in the latest fashion. A strong tornado wind wouldn't be able to upset my hairdo. He was dressed in a suit and tie and his hair was a little long, curly and combed loosely back. He looked so confident sauntering toward me with a friend in tow. I stood a little bit taller.

"Hello, there," he said. "I . . ." His confidence appeared to have reached its maximum hold and he seemed to deflate before my eyes.

"Yes?" I asked. He was visibly flustered; I didn't know what to think and I was willing to help him out only so much.

He cleared his throat and used his fingers to relieve some of the tension his tie was causing.

"Can I help you with something?"

A man came up beside him clapped him on the back and said, "Ma'am. Let me introduce you to my friend here. His name is Peter and it appears you have rendered him mute."

I turned to look at him. His face was beet red and he had trouble making eye contact with me.

"I daresay. I didn't know I possessed that ability," I said smiling, trying to put him at ease. They were both fantastically good-looking, but the shy one—Peter—had a pull on me. I don't know what it was about him that riveted me so; but I didn't want to, nor could I look away.

"Right before we walked in, he was telling me that he now believes in love at first sight," his friend said.

My eyes searched Peter's face.

"Oh, really? Why is that?" I asked lowering my lashes in what I intended to be a chic, coquettish move.

"Because I saw you," he whispered after finding his voice.

And I remember thinking, *Oh boy, that's the best you could come up with?* But he was, again, fantastically good-looking and I was interested. So I smiled to encourage him.

His friend gave him a good shake of the shoulders and excused himself, having done his duty of helping out his buddy. Peter stood there a little awkwardly, but once we started talking a nice conversation ensued. We established we were both from the area and he told me he liked to play guitar, which intrigued me more since I'd always had a crush on musicians. Especially ones who played guitar. Before I knew it, we had a date for the weekend. After that first date, we continued seeing each other frequently and then we went dancing and my life changed.

That was the first time.

***

Peter finally walks in as I'm taking the lasagna out of the oven. How I wish he would walk over and kiss me. I know, I know—wishful thinking on my part. I'm such a hopeless romantic. My heart deflates just a tad bit more. I suppress my disappointment, sigh and think that I should really quit devouring romance novels every time I get a chance, but that's my love fix. I'm a romance addict and I don't care for rehab. Those novels help me get that butterfly-in-my-stomach feeling all over again. They give me something to look forward to. They make me believe that love still exists. That, at least for some, it's not extinct. That maybe one day we—or I—can find it again.

Although that letter from today . . . I stop my thoughts with a screech, and go through the process of setting our plates on the table and we sit. I reprimand myself. How can I possibly allow myself to think of that letter with my husband sitting in front of me? I feel so deliciously unfaithful and so ridiculously guilty. Then I chide myself because I can't be termed unfaithful since I'm not involved with anyone. I'm not meeting anyone and I'm definitely not sleeping with someone else, so technically I'm good, right? But, boy, can that man write.

"The weather sure did turn, huh?" Peter says interrupting my frenzied thoughts.

"Huh?" I mumble letting my thoughts get away from me for a second. I don't want to talk about the weather, I'm daydreaming here! I want to yell, exasperated, but instead I stab my lasagna. I take a bite of what is supposed to taste like tomato sauce, cheese and pasta, but instead of food it seems like my mouth has been filled with stale sadness. Swallowing through the lumps in my throat I eat across from my un-romantic, un-suspecting husband.

***

The next day I'm at work and I swear all I'm doing is rearranging papers on my desk without a specific purpose in sight. My mind is busy. I now work at the public library with three others; Nina, Zach and Marjorie. Marjorie has been here the longest. I think she even helped fund this library. (Could be a slight exaggeration on my behalf.) She moves slowly due to her age and the effects of knee reconstruction surgery, but she's the sweetest person I know. She wears big glasses that reach the middle of her plump cheeks, she smiles with her whole face and her laugh is infectious. She's everyone's grandma and she loves apple blossom flowers, lavender-scented candles and chocolate cake. The more chocolate, the better.

She lost her husband to what she calls a "freak accident," and she's never remarried. Even now at age sixty-six she receives offers; but she says no one can replace her George. They never had children and I find it endearing that she still blushes when she talks about how they tried. Of course, Zach is never around when she talks about *that.*

Sometimes she'll ask me when I'm going to have a baby. I know she means well, she loves babies, and I used to think about what it would be like to have a baby of my own. But how could I possibly bring a child into the folds of a cold family? If only things were different . . . but they're not. And I don't think they'll ever be. I sigh.

It's now ten minutes 'til ten and several mothers walk in with their little ones in tow. Story Time with Marjorie is coming up. Marjorie makes her way to the back room, that's set up for this special time, and several children follow her radiating excitement. No one can make a book come alive quite like Marjorie. She doesn't just read a story; she *becomes* the story with her chameleonic voice and minimal props. She *is* Rapunzel or Snow

White or Rumpelstiltskin. She fights dragons and saves damsels in distress; she sings with forest animals and flies with fairies. The kids love it, as do I.

The children take off their jackets, gloves and scarves and take their places on the floor mat waiting for today's story treat. Then in comes my favorite child, Ralph. He walks in on his mobility aid crutches, which he needs due to cystic fibrosis. But that's not what you notice first. The first thing you see is how grandly he smiles. He uses his whole face to let you know how excited he is to see you. His eyes become animated behind his lopsided glasses, which are held in place by a green retention cord. His tiny freckles are accentuated by the chill that crossed them while he was outside and his hair, which gave in to the wind, is standing haphazardly on his head. There's never been a better-looking kid to me. I go around the counter to give him a hug.

"Mar, Mar, Maaaargie," he stutters in his pure, squeaky voice.

"She's waiting for you," I whisper in his ear.

He turns to find her and if his smile could get any bigger I think it would. He tries to wave; his mom reaches out to support him and then tenderly guides him to Marjorie, who patiently waits for him to take his place on the mat.

"Hello Ralph," says Marjorie. "Are you ready for a story?"

He nods vigorously and smiles.

"Great, let's begin," she says with a smile and a wink. She holds up today's book, reads the title and with a flourish she opens it to the first page.

Before Breakfast

"Where's Papa going with that ax?" said Fern to her mother as they were setting the table for breakfast . . ."

. . .

Marjorie is now Fern from *Charlotte's Web*.

PETER

Today I learned that I have cancer. After everything else that's gone wrong in my life, it almost seems fitting. I deserve a slow, agonizing death, although I wish it would come quickly. The doctor predicts that I have between three to six months left, if I'm lucky. Ha! Lucky! As I'm trying to process this, his words slice and dice through my thoughts.

"It's far too advanced . . . spread to other parts of your body . . . a couple of options to help add some time . . ."

I had cut him off. "Time? Are you talking years with quality of life?" I asked somewhat cynically.

He shook his head sadly. I could tell that giving me this diagnosis was not an easy thing for him. "Months," he responded.

"That's not enough time," I murmured. Then I walked out of his office sucker-punched and stabbed in the back by life.

***

The most natural thing to do when you're told you're going to die is to reflect. The mind wants to analyze memories and compartmentalize. It wants to hold on.

The first thing I need to dissect is my marriage. When I first met Liana, I was certain that I would never have a chance with her; but by some random stroke of luck, she accepted me. I told myself that I wasn't worthy of her; but she made me feel important, valued and loved. Those feelings were hard for me to accept, because after my mother died, I had allowed my heart to close. I convinced myself that if I didn't open up completely, loss couldn't be felt so deeply. I was going through life, alone and cautious.

But, after Liana showed interest in me, I talked myself into thinking that I could have a strong, loving relationship. However, my conviction didn't last long. For the most part, I've been insecure in my ability to love and I've taken her for granted. I love her to the point where I ache but I am too stupid to show her. My tongue is too clumsy to form words befitting the love that my heart feels. I'm a surfer trying to navigate tenuous waters without a surfboard, a hunter without the proper skills, a mechanic without the knack.

I really don't have an excuse as to why I am the way that I am, although, in reality, I probably do. I grew up on a farm on the outskirts of Colorado, in a little town called Skedaddle. The population back then was around fifteen-hundred without counting the drifters, or the people who lived in the woods and didn't want to be counted. And, of course, there was never an official census on the livestock.

My mother was a God-fearing woman, and she always read to me from the Good Book. She baked apple pies, made cheese from scratch, and could wring a chicken's neck without batting an eye. She was a country girl with class. If I could've had her with me a little longer, maybe, just maybe, I would've turned out a little bit better.

But it wasn't meant to be. The spring I was set to turn eleven, my mother went into labor while my father and I were tending the fields. She didn't have anyone with her because she was still two months away from her due date and, as far as anyone was concerned, the pregnancy was pretty normal.

At noon, my father and I headed home for lunch, just like any other day, but this particular day will always be engraved in my mind. No matter what I do, I will never be able to forget the image of my mother on the kitchen floor, blood pooling around her.

"Call the doctor!" my father yelled the moment he saw her. He didn't run toward her, he went in the opposite direction. The phone was on the kitchen counter so I had to go around her. I was close enough to notice that she was still breathing, although it was slow and labored. Sweat was beaded on her forehead, upper lip and neck.

Not once did I take my eyes off of my momma. My father came rushing back in with a pile of towels. He knelt beside her, picked her head up gently and placed a folded towel underneath her neck as I asked the dispatcher to get someone out there quickly. "Please," I pleaded.

The person I was talking to said something I couldn't understand. It was like I was trying to connect letters to make words that in turn would make sound that was supposed to make sense. And I've never been good at playing word games.

"Hello . . . hello? Are you still there?"

I jolted out of my stupor. "Yes, I'm here. Where are they?"

"They're on the way. Ok?"

I nodded, as if she could see me, and then hung up.

My legs were stuck to the floor. My eyes were glued to my mother's face. She looked peaceful. No traces of pain.

By that point my father had placed blankets around her, which were soaking up what they could, and he had also tried to clean up some of the blood, but what was left was smeared in uneven lines on the hardwood floor. It almost looked like someone had been repainting the floor red. I didn't like it. In fact; I hated it.

We were both at a loss about what to do. Thankfully we didn't have to wait too long before I heard tires in our driveway and I hurried to open the door. A small army of people in scrubs was headed toward our house. I opened the door wider letting them in, all the while praying that she would be okay.

I watched as they surrounded my mother and talked amongst each other. I strained to see what they were doing and then I heard my mother mumbling. It sounded like she had said my name, or maybe it was what I wanted to hear, and I was flooded with relief. I wanted to go to her but my father kept me away. He pushed me out onto the porch and I felt like I was being shooed, like a little dog when you no longer want him around. And then he closed the door.

After minutes that felt like hours my father stepped outside. His hair was a savage mess and his eyes darted around insanely, unable to focus on anything, or unwilling to do so. I had never seen him so frazzled.

I sat on our porch swing and waited. I could hear movement inside and I was anxious to find out what was happening. I was tired of not being able to help and my legs were agitated from the inability to run to my mother's side. But yet, there I was sitting and waiting, wearing my fingers raw with the wringing of my hands. Finally, I had to sit on them.

At last an EMT emerged. He looked like a celery stalk with glasses. I hated celery. Looking at my father he slightly shook his head before heading to the ambulance. My father put both his hands to his face and moaned. I went toward the door but another man held me back. I lost it.

"Momma, momma!" I shouted and struggled to get away. "Momma!" I yelled as loud as I possibly could. My eyes spilled tears uncontrollably and my voice caught in my throat that felt like it had been lined with sand. It hurt to scream but she needed to hear me. She needed to know I was there.

I gave up the struggle. I didn't have a chance against that tall, robust, bear-of-a-man. Exhausted, impotent and angry I violently shrugged away from him. I tried to give him the most hateful look I could manage but all he did was look at me with pity. I hated him. He gently moved me to the side and helped Celery Guy carry in a stretcher.

I looked to my father, who was still covering his face and was shaking with the force of his tears. Why wasn't he doing anything? Why didn't he go to her? I wanted to yell at him but instead I could only look at him bewildered. I witnessed how his grief ripped through him and mine threatened to tear me apart. I had never known a heart could hurt so much.

I couldn't sit still any longer. So I ran. Down the front steps and across our yard, as quickly as my thin legs could go. I stopped in front of our big oak tree and started throwing rocks at it. I threw and threw until my arm was sore, as if I had pitched all six innings in a little league game, and then I questioned the sky as I fell to my knees.

"Why, why, why?" I bawled over and over until my throat was drained and the streaks of tears on my face began to dry stiff.

I heard a noise behind me and turned to see Bear Man and Celery Guy rolling my mother out of the house. The other scrubs followed. She was completely covered with a blanket and I began to walk toward her. I tried to reach her before they put her in the back of the ambulance, but I didn't make it. They took her away. I never got to see her again or hear her voice. I didn't get to say goodbye.

***

Even now when I think about that day, my heart is surrounded with sadness, constricted with grief. My father never talked about her again, as if she had never been. I managed to save a photograph of her when I saw him getting rid of her things. He wanted to forget. I wanted to remember.

I can't say that our relationship suffered after we buried my mother. We never really had a strong bond. We didn't play catch, or work on science projects together, or roasted marshmallows in our backyard. I was like a hired worker to him, although I worked for free.

He took up heavy smoking and drinking, and he turned mean. When something went wrong it was because I messed it up. If dinner burnt while he cooked it, why wasn't I watching it? If the dog chewed his shoes, why hadn't I picked them up? And if Mother Nature affected our crop, well, somehow that was my fault too.

I was a failure and he didn't mind letting me know. But what I still can't forgive are the beatings. The ones he inflicted on me because he was mad at the world and I was young, scrawny and available. Anything worked: his boots, his fist, his belt, a switch or a hose. It didn't matter what he used, as long as I was hurt. I couldn't wait to grow up, knock him around a bit and leave.

I never did get around to beating him up. A few days after my fifteenth birthday I decided I was grown and left.

***

A couple of years go by with me barely making ends meet. I did a lot of hard labor tending fields, working on a dairy and caring for livestock. That was what I knew how to do and what gave me a roof over my head. I constantly felt sorry for myself, and then one day . . . a stroke of luck.

I drove into town to purchase feed. As I walked down Main Street, I happened to glance inside the JC Penney store window and saw a vision in white. My heart sped up and my feet got tangled with each other, causing me to trip. As my face got closer to the sidewalk, someone caught me, saving me from catastrophic embarrassment.

"You all right there, mate?" I heard a man say in a very exaggerated Pirate's drawl.

I looked up to see who had saved me and noticed someone about my age, who was extremely well dressed. Looking at his face I could tell that he was working awfully hard to suppress a laugh. So, I put him out of his misery. I busted out laughing and he joined me wholeheartedly. Once we are able to get a grip, he introduced himself.

"Joseph Whittle, mate," he said shaking my right hand and clapping me on the back with his left.

"Peter Hartsfield," I replied still smiling.

"Are you from around here?"

"From Skedaddle, and you?

"My father owns land there. I'm actually coming home so he can show me the ways of the business, so I can take over the company—or be ready to—type stuff." He shrugs and adds, "Pretty boring, if you ask me. Anyhoo, where are you headed?"

"To the Hokum Feed Store. My boss wants me to pick up medicines and feed."

"Do you have time to get a sandwich? I was just on my way to the deli, and I'd be honored if you would join me."

My heart was deeply affected. I had dirt on me from my toenails to my lashes—I couldn't tell if I was wearing it or it was wearing me—but there he was asking me to lunch. I was about to turn him down when my stomach launched a growling solo, deciding for me.

"Well, I guess that's settled," he teased, laughing again.

Side by side we headed to the deli and not once did he seem ashamed to be walking by my disheveled, stinky self. I couldn't stop smiling. Once outside the deli, I tried to pound off as much dirt as I could from my clothes.

"Don't worry about it," said Joseph as he opened the door. "It adds character."

Once inside I headed directly to the bathroom. I might've had character, but I wasn't about to eat without washing my hands. I could at least pretend to be decent. I washed my hands and face, dried off and somewhat satisfied I went back out to the dining area, which was now fuller than when we had first entered.

We ordered club sandwiches with double meat, French fries and Cokes. I racked my brain trying to find a suitable conversation, but I shouldn't have worried, he had one ready as we sat.

"So, Peter. What had you so distracted back there?"

I blushed and took a long drink instead of answering.

Reading into my silence he questioned, "Have you talked to her?"

I shook my head and was saved from having to say anything else by our waitress. She set our sandwiches in front of us and asked if we needed anything else. When Joseph told her that we were fine she hesitated for a few seconds before turning to leave, visibly disappointed. He didn't seem to notice; instead he started eating his fries several at a time. I glanced to the counter and found the waitress gawking at him and then turned back to Joseph who hadn't given her a second thought. I shrugged, covered my fries in ketchup and started eating.

"So, you work on a dairy, which I find super interesting," he said with a pronounced eye roll. "What do you do for fun?"

"Nothing really," I replied, wincing at the reality of my boring existence. "Sometimes I go fishing."

"Good, that's something I can work with. How about we go this coming Saturday? Will you have the day off?"

"Actually, I will—half a day, anyway."

"What lake do you go to?"

"Lake Zillah. It has the best trout you could ever hope to catch."

"Great! Where do we meet?"

"Take the Shady Hill Road all the way to its end and you'll see my truck. My boss has a small boat that he lets me use. It's nothing fancy though," I explained.

"Four o'clock sound good?"

"That's fine."

We finished our food in silence. Sandwich bites and fries going in at the same time.

I looked at the clock on the wall and realized I needed to get back to work.

"I gotta go," I said digging into my pockets for a few bills to cover my meal.

"Don't worry about it. It's my treat."

"You don't have to do that," I protested.

"It's okay. Really. You'll get the next one."

"Sounds like a plan," I said picking up my trash and turning toward the door. "See you Saturday."

"See you then, mate," he replied. "And, by the way . . . you should talk to her," he added, holding up his last fry and pointing it at me.

I laughed and walked away. Once outside I ventured another glance into the diner and I found the waitress stretching to follow Joseph's movements as he's readying

to leave. I shook my head and, still smiling, headed to
the feed store.

LIANA

'm in the process of re-shelving books, pulling and tugging a loaded book cart with me, on the library's second floor, when I hear a few gasps and murmurs drifting up from the lobby. I peer over the banister and watch as Nina stands there; her boyfriend of two years, Matthew, kneeling before her. I can't hear what he is saying but I can take a wild guess. I'm so enthralled by the scene that I don't think to get closer. And then she yelps a piercing, "YES!" He places a ring on her finger and a collective cheer goes up as he stands and embraces her.

I realize I'm crying, emotional weakling that I am, so I head to the bathroom to compose myself. On my way all I can hear are the congratulatory shrieks coming from below. I can't wait to close the door behind me and when I finally do: blissful silence.

***

I think back to my own wedding proposal. That day we had gone to the drive in and ate greasy burgers, onion rings and double chocolate milkshakes as we watched a movie. The name of the movie escapes me because of what happened afterward.

As Peter was driving me home, we were quietly cutting through the night. Rain had started falling and fat drops slapped the windshield relentlessly. We reached my house and I turned to kiss him goodnight, but he was looking straight ahead lost in his thoughts.

"Peter?" I asked reaching for his arm.

"You know, I've been thinking," he started.

"Oh yeah? About what?"

"That we should get married."

He said this without a glance toward me.

My jaw dropped along with my hand. This isn't how I had envisioned a proposal at all. Whatever happened to a lavishly set dinner at an expensive restaurant with a ring hidden in the dessert, or a star-studded walk in the park with a ring glinting in the moonlight, or a ridiculously large bouquet of roses with a ring box in his pocket; that I had read—and dreamed about—time and time again?

I was so stunned—and somewhat disappointed— that I didn't say anything, and finally he turned to me.

"What do you say?" he asked. His hands were wearing the steering wheel senseless, he was so nervous.

"Are you being serious?" My voice came out in an airy breath. I couldn't believe what was going on.

"Yes. Yes, I am," he answered, his voice gaining a little ground. Then he smiled at me and my heart dissolved. The rain outside stopped as if it too was waiting for my response.

"Okay then," I said. "Yes."

"Really?" he asked.

"You sound surprised," I responded smiling.

"No. No. Not surprised. I'm . . ." He exhaled. "Oh my God. I'm just so . . . so happy." Then he released the steering wheel and we joined in an awkward embrace in the tight space afforded by his small, black Ford truck.

That was my proposal. I said yes, and I didn't even get a ring.

***

"Liana, are you in here?" I hear Marjorie ask.

"Just a minute," I say in a false chipper voice. I clear my throat and flush the toilet, making time. Maybe she'll leave.

"I wanted to let you know that there's cake in the break room to celebrate Matthew and Nina's engagement. Did you see it?"

"See what?"

"The proposal."

"No, I didn't," I lie. Why, I'm not exactly sure. "I'll be right there."

Since she doesn't leave I can't postpone my exit from the stall any longer. I walk out and head toward the sink, purposefully avoiding her look and my reflection in the mirror. But I must be a real sight because she gasps.

"Honey, are you okay?"

Instead of responding I look up to face myself in the mirror. I see a red nose, flushed cheeks and puffy eyes. Oh, no. I can't tell her I've been crying, much less why. How can I explain away my face? *Think, think,* I tell myself. Then it comes to me. With a slightly shaky hand, I touch my forehead, "I don't know," I start. "I do feel a little under the weather, like I might be coming down with something."

She comes toward me. "Here, let me see." She puts the back of her hand to my forehead. "You do feel a little warm. I have Tylenol. I'll go get it."

"No," I say a little too hastily. She turns and gives me a curious look. "It's okay. I have some in my purse. I'll take those."

"Do you want me to bring you your purse?" she asks heading back out the door.

"No, thank you. I'm headed that way now." I walk past her, embarrassed because I saw in her face that she didn't believe me. If I had joined the One-Act play back in high school, when I'd been asked, maybe my histrionics would be somewhat more credible.

***

Today is my day to close. It's been incredibly busy and there's so much to do; too bad I now have an unreasonable headache. I call Peter, ask him what he wants for dinner and grimace as soon as I hear Elton John in the background singing "I Guess That's Why They Call It the Blues," which means he's in one of his melancholic moods. I tense even more and feel the strain of it in my neck and shoulders. I ask him if Chinese is okay, while trying to rub my tension away. He says that's fine and we hang up.

There was a time when life had been easy. When decisions weren't complicated. Where there were only white and black areas, no gray. How I wish now that I hadn't tried so hard to grow up quickly back then. I could spend hours in my backyard playing in the dirt, twirling in the swing that my father had hung from a sturdy oak tree, or chasing the neighbor's cat (since I wasn't allowed to have my own). My mother was allergic, or at least that's the story I got.

I was care-free, unburdened by life, unaware of disappointments. I was a princess and my wishes were truth. I don't want to say I was spoiled, but I guess I'd be lying if I said that I wasn't.

I remember sitting cross-legged in the yard sharing a Hershey bar with my father, while my mother hung laundry or finished up one chore or another. I knew she loved me. They both adored me. I was their surprise after they'd come to terms with the possibility of never being able to have children. They were in their mid-forties when I showed up and nothing had ever been too much for me.

And, the biggest question now could be, why I don't run to my loving parents for help or advice about my marriage. The short and simple answer to that, if there ever was one, is that I don't want to be a failure in their eyes. Their marriage is solid and full of love. I can't let them see that I'm miserable, disappointed and on the verge of giving up. Plus, they've never been crazy about my husband; especially my mother. She seems to believe that Peter ruined my chances of "getting what I deserved." That because of him I will "never reach my full potential." As if all of life depended on finding the right man to make a woman worthy of living.

Therefore, I've never told her my misgivings or troubles with Peter. Not because I don't trust her, but because I want her to like him. Besides, he's not a monster, he's just not affectionate. I realize that's not a crime, but it is disheartening. And a girl needs love. Not just the physical kind—the soul kind.

I do realize that if I leave Peter, my parents will inevitably have to know. If my best friend, Daisy, were in town, I could stay with her for a while. Only until Peter and I found our way back to each other, and then my parents would never have to know that there was a glitch in my marriage. But Daisy's off seeing the world with her new boyfriend, some oil magnate. I can't even think of his name right now.

So my leaving will have to wait. Not just because she's not here; but also because I do still love him, even when I don't. Crazy, huh? Maybe the solution could be to take some time off from "us". The "make him see what he's missing" type of time off. I'm not talking about seeing other people. Or maybe I am.

I keep going back to my letter:

"If you need a walk in the rain, let me take that walk with you. If you need a cry alongside a riverbank, let me be your shoulder to cry on. If you need to make a wish upon a star, let me be the one that finds the star that will make your wish come true."

I do have a wish. I want to be happy.

I could try to find out who sent it and take it from there. He said he likes to stroll downtown. Maybe I could go there and observe the crowds. Maybe I'll be able to feel him when I see him.

I shake my head vigorously, as if trying to dislodge and expel these crazy thoughts. What am I thinking? I can't go on a wild-goose chase; it's crazy! I know. I haven't even made up my mind to leave Peter and I'm already thinking of the what-ifs.

If I keep going back and forth on my decision I'll never act, one way or the other. Time is getting away from me. I have to make up my mind. I pause, take a deep breath and as I exhale the only thought that I have is that I'm going to tell him we need some time. I'll work out the details later.

***

"I heard you weren't feeling well. Are you better?" Zach asks as he steps behind the counter, pushing his glasses back up his nose.

"Yes, thank you," I say. "The Tylenol really helped," although I never took them, but he doesn't need to know that.

"Good. So, what did you think about Matthew?"

"I didn't see him," I say. "What about him?" I really don't want to talk about this, so I start picking up books that need to be checked back in and scanning them.

"How he dressed up as Prince Charming."

"Is that what he did? I guess that's sweet," I say

wanting to change the subject.

"I'm sure she'll be planning a fairy tale wedding."

"Those are her favorite stories," I say and it's here that I find my chance for a new conversation. "Speaking of stories, did we get the new *Stuart Little* book?"

"We sure did. I already put it on the counter in back with Ralph's name on it."

I smile. That Ralphie sure does have a way with our hearts. "He's gonna love it," I say.

A man, who looks to be in his early thirties, walks up to the counter with his hands full of books, ready to be checked out. He comes in regularly and he's always very polite.

Once, I watched him walk in with the ladies of the Serenity Assisted Living Home; who come in, usually every other Thursday, and he was pushing one of them in her wheelchair. I hadn't seen that particular lady before. She was thin with a puff of white hair; her neck couldn't hold her head up straight anymore, but her eyes were spirited. She wore pink lipstick and small pearl earrings; a white top stamped with a rainbow of flowers and white bottoms. I could tell she wasn't a sad old lady.

When I was checking her out, he teased her about her selections.

"*A Gentleman of Sorts, The Pirate's Lady, A Lover for Sunday?*" He gasped. "What kind of stories are you reading

Mrs. Bertie?" he asked fondly, raising his eyebrows at her.

She smiled at him, as a thin blush colored her wrinkled cheeks. "Oh, stop it," she countered, her voice cheerful. "A woman my age can still have a little romance in her life. I have to keep this ticker going—one way or another," she joked, pointing to her chest.

"I've already told you all you have to do is ask. My heart is yours," he told her as he bent over her hand and placed a soft kiss on it.

"Oh, hush," she laughed, basking in his attention. "You're no pirate, or duke, or . . ."

"Gentleman?" he finished for her, with mock indignation.

She harrumphed. "If I was younger and not trapped by this wheelchair, young man, you wouldn't have a chance of running."

"If you were younger, Mrs. Bertie, I wouldn't even try to run," he told her.

She turned to look at me. "You see what I have to put up with? This boy here's gonna be the sweet death of me."

"Is that right?" I asked as I stashed her books in her bag.

"I'm serious. He's the sweet-talking kind that can get a girl all flustered, and then they don't know what to do when their hearts get serious. You gotta watch his kind."

"I see," I replied, laughing and stealing a glance at him.

"Now, before you continue talking bad about me to this nice lady," he jumped in, "I think we should get you back to your room so you can get started on those "nice" books of yours."

She patted his hand affectionately when he gave her her bag. "Yes! On to the world of Pirates, chiseled abs, and steamy romances," she said, raising her fist as in victory.

Giggling I thanked her. He shrugged happily, and exaggeratedly rolled his eyes.

***

"I hear you guys got quite a show today," he says, and I jump back into the present.

"Excuse me?"

"The proposal," he explains and when he smiles there's a conspiratorial, flirty glint in his eyes.

"Where you here?" I ask surprised. "That happened quite a few hours ago."

"No, I wasn't. It was on the news, '*Librarian gets fairy tale proposal*'. It was quite a heart-throbbing thing to witness —and to be surrounded by books full of stories, poems, letters . . ." he trails off and smiles at me once again.

My stomach inadvertently drops and my mind begins spinning, wondering if this could be my secret admirer. Why is he looking at me like that? Is he flirting with me?

I clear my throat. "Did you find everything you were looking for?" I ask ready to get him out of here, since I can feel myself becoming a little unnerved by his presence; and remembering how much I had liked him the last time I'd seen him hadn't helped matters.

He looks at me intently and says, "Yes. I think I did."

I look away quickly and reach for his library card. His fingers graze mine, surprising me and causing me to drop it. Did he do that on purpose?

"Forgive me," he says bending to retrieve the card. "I can be so clumsy at times."

"It's fine, no worries," I say as I reach for the card again, this time careful not to touch him. Inside I'm yelling at myself to get it together. I'm not a young, innocent girl of eighteen given to temporary crushes. I'm a married woman for goodnessake! I scan his card and the information on the screen tells me he's Malcolm Hawthorn, from over on Riverside, which is the really good side of town.

"How's Mrs. Bertie?" I ask trying to calm my nerves.

"She's doing great. She's somewhere on the Caribbean with a pirate named Hugo," he pantomimes, covering one of his eyes. "Who is now the love of her life." He sighs as if heart-broken.

So much for safer territory. I forgot she reads steamy romances. I look for another angle. Surely *he* doesn't read romance. "What do you like to read?"

"I'm actually doing research for a book I'm writing."

"Really?" I squeak. Oh my God! He's a writer? Then it hits me full-force. HE'S A WRITER!—and he's flirting with me. It's got to be him. I'm so ruffled, I can barely hear the beeping of the scanner over the beating my chest is taking from my heart.

"What kind of book?" I ask cautiously, not really wanting to know the answer. But one can't go without asking a writer what they're writing, once they've shared that they have an on-going project.

"Romance," he responds matter-of-factly. And now I'm sure I'm going to faint. I can feel his gaze pouring through me. I look at the book I'm holding. It's a collection of classical poetry. It falls out of my trembling hand.

"Are you okay?" he asks, reaching out to me.

I step back, shaking my head ever-so-slightly. I can't let him touch me. He gives me a look I can't decipher; something between concern and attraction. I look away.

Zach comes to my aid. "Here, Liana, let me help you with this; you go sit down."

"Thanks," I murmur and stagger to the back.

"She hasn't been feeling well all day," I hear Zach explain as I'm retreating.

"Hmm. Must be the weather," Malcolm responds,

his voice silky smooth. I can feel his eyes following me.

**

Once I hear Zach wishing Malcolm a good evening and happy reading, I venture back toward the door. I want one more glimpse. As he's walking past the return window, he happens to look back at the same time I sneak a glance. Our eyes meet, he winks and smiles, and I swoon. Literally, like in the novels. I use my hand to steady myself as I duck back into the safety of the back room. Un-freaking-believable! Could I have been any more forward? Or obvious?

"What was that all about?" Zach asks as he enters the room, scratching his head full of unruly, red curls.

"What do you mean?"

"Is something going on with Malcolm?"

"No, why would you think that?" I ask and hurry to add, "You know I'm married and I would not cheat on Peter." I wince hearing the word cheat coming out of my mouth. I'm not being accused of that and here I am putting the thought out there.

He throws his hands up, "Hey! No one's saying you're cheating. I was only curious." He raises his eyebrows to me. "He is handsome and sweet and seems taken with you. Would you ever consider it?"

Why is he asking me this? I shake my head, maybe

not as vigorously as I should. I don't even know if I'm trying to convince Zach or myself now. And I'm not sure why I'm even trying to explain myself to Zach. He's not married. He doesn't know my story. He has a mysterious girlfriend who none of us have met and, who conveniently lives in another town. That doesn't make him a relationship expert.

So instead of giving him another affirmation of my impending infidelity or unfailing devotion I just say, "You know I haven't felt good all day," and shiver for effect.

"Riiiiiiight," he responds. "Then you should probably take the day off tomorrow so you can cure what ails you."

"I just might do that," I say, and he turns and walks away leaving me with my nervous self. If only one day could be enough to cure what ails me.

PETER

How does a person comprehend the magnitude of a death sentence? What is the rational way to process the news? How do you manage the influx of emotions? How do you tell yourself you're going to die?

After leaving the doctor's office I drive and drive unable to stop my tears and fears. I don't understand. Why me? Why now? I had a full life planned with Liana and eventually our children. Now I have to change all of that. I need to prepare everything so my passing will cause minimal impact to my wife.

And there's also someone else I need to see. Not for his sake . . . for mine.

***

As I near the house, I see proof that he's no longer alone. A plump snowman sits in the front yard with its carrot nose, licorice-red lips, hat, and pink scarf. A miniature snowman is beside it; their stick hands intertwined. I feel a stirring in my chest and it hurts.

I pull into the driveway and kill my truck. I sit there for a few minutes, mustering courage. After realizing I won't have more than what I came with, I exit my truck and walk to the front door. I raise my hand to knock, but before I can make contact, I hear running and yelling coming from inside, followed by laughter. Deciding I can't go through with this, I turn to leave. As I'm about to take my first steps away from the door, it opens.

Two little girls stand before me in jackets and boots, and their eyes go wide with surprise and curiosity. Apparently they were headed outside and can't figure out what to do with me standing there. As we look at each other, all of us trying to decide, I hear a woman's voice coming from inside, instructing them to close the door.

"You're letting the cold in," she continues, her voice getting closer. Then she is before me; my father's wife.

"Oh," she says, surprised to see me. "Can I help you?" she asks, and quickly puts her arms around both of the girls. Protecting them.

I try to speak, but I can't. I am shocked with her beauty. She's of average height about 5'7" or 5'8". Not skinny, but definitely not fat. She has a head full of burgundy wavy hair flowing around her face and over her shoulders. Her eyes are an impossible gray-green hue, outlined in black. A spattering of freckles is scattered across her nose and cheekbones. Her smile is so big, glossy, red and easy, it's welcoming. Her thin eyebrows raise a little, waiting for me to speak.

I finally find my voice. "Hi." I stammer. "I'm . . ." I clear my throat. "I'm looking for Charles Hartsfield. I'm . . ."

"Peter," she says, cutting me off.

I nod, surprised she knows of me. "You know me?"

"Charles has mentioned you, a time or more, and we have a picture. You were much younger there, so it took me a minute to see it. Charles is out back, in the garage. Is he expecting you?" Her voice isn't guarded. I can tell she's one of those people that like everyone instantly and have a hard time disliking someone, even if they've given them reason to.

"No."

"No matter. I was just brewing some coffee to take out there. Would you like some?" she asks fully opening the door to me.

Tentatively I step inside my childhood home and am instantly flooded with memories. My mother singing, cooking, baking and then lying on the kitchen floor. I start to shake and then feel a hand on my arm.

"Are you okay? Would you like to sit down?" Her voice is soothing with a dash of country smoothness to enrich it.

I nod and she guides me to the couch. I feel like a fool, allowing my emotions to control me so easily. She sends the oldest girl to get a glass of water while the youngest clings to her side.

"I'm Vivian," she says. "This is Brae," and upon the other girl's return she introduces her as Eden. I register the beeps of a coffee machine finishing its cycle and she smiles at me, that easy smile, flashing her perfect white teeth. I decide right then that I like her. Eden hands me the glass of water, which I accept and drink from out of courtesy.

"Nice to meet you," I tell all three. The girls give me polite, shy smiles.

"Let me get that coffee and you can take it out to him," Vivian tells me, and instructs the girls to go back out and play. "I'll call you back in as soon as lunch is ready," she says, as the girls head out the door, throwing quick glances my way, and then they're gone. Vivian turns to me. "You'll join us, right?" It is more a statement than a question and I can't say no. With that, she turns for the kitchen, and I am left all alone in the family room. As alone as a person can be with ghosts.

I turn and take in my surroundings. The walls are generously furnished with pictures. And smiles. I can almost hear the happiness. Then I look to the fireplace mantelpiece and I see her; my mom. I stand to get a better look. There she is, and she has her arms around me. Tears escape me. He didn't forget.

I hear footsteps behind me, and I wipe my face before I turn. At any other point in my life I would've probably been furious at my father for moving on and marrying again, but today (after the doctor put life in perspective for me), I understand, and I'm glad he did.

Vivian hands me two coffee mugs. "Here. He'll be happy to see you," she affirms.

I wouldn't be so sure, I think, but instead of voicing my thoughts I turn away from her. With a shaky disposition, I head out the door and walk to the garage in the back yard. I feel like a little child being told to look into the closet to ensure that monsters aren't real. The child can see an empty closet, but the fear is still there. I, too, am anxious and I don't want to face this; but I feel Vivian's eyes following me, so I keep walking.

As I get nearer, I hear the music of my early years. The Beatles', "Twist and Shout" fills the space and makes it cheerful. How my mother had loved that music! I remember she would make me dance with her, if I happened by, and I would act embarrassed. But, in truth, I loved every one of those moments with her.

Instead of making my presence known right away, I observe my father for a beat. He's bent over the engine of the 1965 Mustang he'd always wanted. He has patches of grease on his work clothes and smeared on his hands and forearms. He straightens and reaches for the rag he keeps in his back pocket, and starts wiping his hands. Then he looks up and sees me.

He's older. I don't know why this strikes me, so am I. His hair has gone from a chestnut brown to gray-white and it's cut short. He now carries a belly that hangs a little over his belt. His eyes look tired.

"Peter," he says and stumbles backward a step or two, as if he can't believe it really is me. He catches himself on the counter.

The song ends and a new one starts. He looks at me, speechless; and in that moment, every blow, every hurtful word heals. I can't hate him anymore. I find it unbelievable how easily I see this truth after years of resentment, of carrying around the pain.

I walk to him and hand him his coffee mug. "Vivian sent you this," I say.

"You met her then?"

I don't respond.

He takes the mug, and lowers the volume on his cassette player. I wish he hadn't. It was Leo Sayer with "You Make Me Feel Like Dancing." Mom often told me the story of how her and Father were at a mutual friend's party one night when this song came on. They had a habit of changing dance partners randomly during songs, and my parents happened to end up together for this one. Their feet matching step for step and the energy hovering around them made them give up changing dance partners. They introduced themselves while dancing and never looked back.

Maybe that's why he lowered the volume. Maybe he remembered too.

I take a sip of the coffee, which is strong, and point to the car. "This yours?"

"Yeah. Just finished the oil change."

"She's a beauty," I say, admiring its shiny exterior. I venture toward it and take a peek inside.

"Would you like to take her for a spin?" he asks.

I look at him, wide-eyed. I can tell how much this car means to him and realize it's his way of apologizing. I walk around to the driver's side but before I can open the door I feel his hand on my shoulder.

"It's good to see you," he says, his voice shaky.

I nod and open the door without looking back. I turn the engine, listening to its beautiful rumble and feeling its energy through my body. I shift it into gear and navigate out of the garage. Out of the corner of the rearview mirror, I see my father wiping his eyes with the back of his hand. I feel my heart shift.

I make my way to the most solitary back road I know, and pick up speed. I'm leaving dust in my wake, and my childhood heartaches scrambled along with it.

***

When I return, I see my father sitting in a rocking chair on his ample porch. Patiently waiting, steadily chewing gum; it suddenly dawns on me that his customary cigarette is gone. He signals for me to leave the car out front. Once I have it in park and the engine off, I get out and walk toward the house.

He stands as I approach. "Vivian has lunch ready," he says, opening the door.

The girls are laughing and playing in the family room, and as soon as I walk in, they both give me curious glances and giggle their way to the dining room. I wonder if they've been told who I am.

Vivian comes in from the kitchen, and says, "I'm almost finished. Everyone get cleaned up, and come find your seat."

I head to the bathroom after commenting on how good it smells. Although, in truth, the smell of the food makes me hungry and nauseous at once. I'll get through it, I tell myself. I wash my hands and face, and then I join them in the dining room.

My father and his new family are already seated at the table. He's at the head, like he always used to, but now he has a daughter on each side and Vivian sitting by the oldest, Eden. I take the chair by Brae.

The spread before me looks almost festive. A dish of steaming pot roast is set beside a tray filled with freshly baked bread. And I'm sure something sweet is waiting for dessert. I can smell it in the air, and suddenly my failing body is ravenous.

I watch as they hold hands, Brae taking one of mine and Vivian reaching out for my other. Then Vivian says a blessing for the food and for each one of us gathered around the table. We take turns giving Vivian our bowls to be filled with thick slices of roast and abundant servings of vegetables. Slices of bread are added to our bread plates, and we all start eating.

After the main course, Vivian brings out a mouthwatering apple crisp, which she serves with scoops of Blue Bell's Homemade Vanilla ice cream. I eat until I feel like I'm going to be sick, but the food was worth it.

When we finish, the girls are sent off to get ready for more outside play and Vivian starts to work on clearing the table. My father stands and heads to the family room and I follow. In awkward silence I sit—without the distraction of a car, or food, or girl's chatter—across from the man that I hated for so long.

My emotions are like an old piece of rope that's lost its grip, and is unraveling—all the different sensations of the day are catching up to me.

"You all right?" he asks, looking directly at me.

I sigh. "I miss her," I say, and just like that we finally cry together (him from his chair, I from mine) for the wonderful woman we lost so long ago and for the choices we made afterwards. Tears slide down our faces as if washing away the regrets.

Once I recover, I look at him and ask, "Have you wondered why I'm here today, after all this time?"

"Of course I have, but I don't really care why. You're here, and that's what matters." He coughs roughly, then adds, "I'm so, so sorry for (another cough) for . . . everything," he says looking away.

I don't respond. I wait for him to look at me again and staring him in the eyes, I slowly shake my head and say, "I'm dying."

***

On my way home, I pass the Skedaddle Cemetery. I've only been there once before, when I watched them lower my mother's coffin, and then cover it with a colossal amount of dirt. My baby brother, who I never got to see, was with her; and soon I would be too.

I pull over, stop the truck, and walk. I'm not exactly sure where their graves are, but I feel a strong pull guiding me, so I follow it. Finally, I see the tombstones. Their tops are covered with snow and my mother's and brother's names are inscribed on the front, with birth and death dates. With my gloved hand, I remove the snow from my mother's gravestone and kneel in front of it. By now I'm crying uncontrollably, and I choke out, "Mom. I'm scared."

I weep until I feel exhausted, and then I think of my wife. How am I going to tell Liana? I rest my forehead on the cold stone, and I feel a calmness come over me. I can't explain it but suddenly I feel strong, determined to make the most out of the time I have left.

Daytime is losing its light. I figure it must be past five so I head for home. On the way, I am more observant of my surroundings. I pass the construction site for the new health food store coming to town. There's a new bride being photographed, outside a church, in the waning light. She looks beautiful in her white dress and has a huge smile plastered on her face. The city park has an expansion project advertised. Everyone is planning their future while I am planning my end.

I pull into my driveway and observe my house. I think of all the hard work I put into being able to afford it. I wanted to have something to offer Liana. Not that she demanded it, but I knew she was used to nice things and I wanted to continue giving them to her.

Looking at the house now, with its sage exterior, rustic brick accents and covered in snow, I notice that it looks lonely. There are no toys strewn about the yard, no lopsided snowmen, or snow angels. The curtains are drawn. There is no light.

As I enter the house, I smell the dinner Liana made and go in search of her. She used to wait for me with a smile and a kiss, always excited to see me. But within my love for her there also lay an awkwardness, a feeling of needing to stay guarded from the possibility of losing her, so I kept her at a distance. I built walls around my heart preventing her from moving completely in. Unintentionally and intentionally I hurt her. What a fool I have been.

I notice a faint light glowing from the enclosed porch. There she is, stretched on the wicker sofa, covered in a blanket, reading. The sight of her takes my breath away. My heart tightens as I watch her. I love her so much and I don't know how to show it. Now that I think about it, she was the first one to say *I love you*, and I responded with a "me too." It's always been the same. It's been a while since she last said it.

A sudden discomfort in my stomach surprises me causing me to gasp.

She looks up, and immediately stands.

"Peter, what's wrong?" she asks, walking toward me.

A wave of nausea hits me and I tumble toward the closest wicker chair. I put my head in my hands and wait for the episode to pass, after all, it's not the first one I've had and I know they're only going to get worse.

"Peter, what's wrong?" Liana asks again.

I look up at her. She's standing there with a glass of water in her hand. I don't recall hearing her leave the porch. She hands it to me and when I try to reach for her hand she doesn't take mine. I almost think I see her flinch. I should be happy, she's detached. That was my intention. To protect us, exactly from what I'm no longer sure, and I also can't understand how I ever thought that was the way to live. I love her with all my might and my time to prove it has been shortened. I start to cry, I feel so broken.

"Peter, you're scaring me. What's going on?" Worry creeps into her voice with a hint of irritation, and I can't talk. Frustrated she turns to leave the room.

I clear my throat. "I have cancer," I say in a gruff whisper.

She stops at the doorway and puts her hand on the doorjamb.

Slowly, she turns back to me. "What did you say?"

I clear my throat again and this time, my voice somewhat firmer, I repeat, "I have cancer."

In disbelief she makes her way to the spot where she had been reading. She sits and the silence that ensues surrounds us like a cloak, one that has become too small to wear comfortably.

I sigh, tired. I look at Liana, who is wiping away the tears that are now inching down her face. She is still breath-taking. I have been a very lucky guy. Her—not so much. She now wears the look of the disappointed, and carries the weight of the let-down. If only life could be built on good-intentions, because I had plenty of those when we were dating.

***

Had it not been for Joseph, I would probably still be only daydreaming about Liana, but he encouraged me and made me feel like I had a shot.

It had been very cold that winter day, four years ago, and I had awoken from a restless sleep. I walked over to the frosty window and looked out over the expansive fields, which were somewhat covered with snow. Bits and pieces of brown grass showed through the white powder, reminding me of an old man who couldn't grow a full beard. And I thought to myself, I don't want to be an old man with a patchy life.

Determined, I put on a pot of coffee, threw on my best clothes, and went in search of my friend. As I ventured into town I passed several snowmen decorating yards. Some were short and plump and some were anorexic, not at all what a normal snowman should look like. Most all had grass and mud showing through their forms, giving them creative uniqueness.

In front of some houses, families played in the snow. Children lay out on the ground, forming snow angels and laughing the day away, while other families were involved in snow-ball fights. All of them wore winter gear; red runny noses and smiles that made me envious. I didn't have recollections of doing things like that with my parents. But there I was, on a mission to make new memories.

I accelerated, feeling my truck protest before it picked up speed, and I tried my best to ignore the happiness around me.

I reached downtown, parked in front of the JC Penney, and waited for Joseph. While I sat there, I turned the radio to 93.5 KPOW, the only station worth listening too. I heard my favorite song, Billy Joel's "You may be right," and I started drumming my fingers on my thigh.

Then, I joined in on the chorus:

"You may be right, I may be crazy
But it just might be a lunatic you're looking for
Turn out the light, don't try to save me
You may be wrong for all I know
But you may be right…"

Immediately, my mood started to lift. That song ended, and Blue Swede followed it with "Hooked on a Feeling," and by then I was giddy, with new hope surging through me. Gotta love the oldies.

Joseph pulled up beside me, we brainstormed, and together we walked into the JC Penney. I lost my nerve, said something totally un-romantic, but she smiled and in that moment I became absolutely, un-deniably hers.

***

In hindsight, I can't figure out what attracted her to me, and I want to kick myself for not having made her as happy as she deserves. And now that I see the error of my way, it's too late.

It truly is going to be my loss, not hers.

LIANA

My mind reels with the three words it tries to register. I look outside, where I immediately focus on the neighbors' Christmas lights, blinking away cheerily, and I feel the urge to rush over there and yank them all out. Then I want to yell at them for being so insensitive.

"Liana." Peter's voice brings me back. I was supposed to talk to him about taking time-off from us. Obviously I can't do that now. What am I going to do? Why is this happening?

I look at him. How could I not have noticed what is so obvious now? He has lost some weight, his skin is somewhat pale, and his eyes . . . I have to look away.

There was a time when I thought I could get lost in those eyes. His gaze was so intense I could feel it reverberate through my body. I never thought I could want for more. But here we are, four years later, two strangers needing to pull together to face a terrible evil.

I still love him. I do, but years of subtle and not-so-subtle rejection have made me somewhat cold. I don't know how deep inside I'll have to search to find the love he needs at this time. I've worked so hard to *not* feel.

He coughs. I let out a long breath and try to arrange my thoughts. There's a myriad of questions going through my mind. Which should I ask first?

I settle with, "Could there be a mistake?"

"No. I received confirmation today from a specialist."

"Is there a cure?" I whisper.

He lets out a sob and shakes his head. "I wish there was," he says. "I really wish there was."

I can't help it. I go to him. I kneel in front of him and put my arms around his neck, and together we cry. The embrace is so awkward, it's perfect.

After a little while he puts his hands on the sides of my face and looks at me. He really *looks* at me and says, "I'm so . . . so sorry I have failed you."

"No," I start. But he stops me with a kiss. Not just a peck, an all-involving kiss. The kind that makes time stop and guilt disappear. The kind of kiss I've read about and longed for. The kind of kiss that makes one senseless and reckless. The kind that makes one dizzy with desire and crazy with abandon.

I am startled by the level of passion this kiss awakens in me, and when he breaks away, I search his face and recognize my feelings mirrored there. I want him in a way I don't understand. My breathing is heavily laced with a yearning that seems to have taken on a life of its own. I want to ask him if it will be okay, if I can have him, but I don't want him to tell me no. I search for, not wanting to find any signs of discomfort; and once I'm satisfied with what I see, I reach for his hand and lead him to our bedroom. I hold back and wait, even though I want to ravage him every step of the way.

In our bedroom, which has been devoid of love-making, we undress each other slowly, enjoying every inch of skin as it's revealed. Although I know his skin, have touched it and tasted it before, tonight it's different. I run my hands along the length of his arms and snake my fingers through his hair, kissing him with all the fervor that I have. He touches me with un-abashed longing and intensity. His breath is a whisper on my skin. He's not in a hurry; he gives me his love and his need like he never has before. It appears that every physical encounter we've had was only a rehearsal leading up to this night.

We fall onto the bed, and I take charge of him—of us. I have no inhibitions. I explore him, like I never have before, propelled with the knowledge that this dance is one that we may never have like this again. All the love I once felt and had tried to bury resurfaces. Looking at him now—right here, right now—I believe in magic and music and the power of our love. I fly.

Afterwards, I lie in his arms, my head on his chest, completely satisfied; and I feel his tears wetting my hair. I hold him tighter and don't speak. We stay like this until our heartbeats return to normal and his breathing evens out.

I fall asleep to the rhythm of his heart, as snow falls delicately outside our window, and wishing that our love could have been as intense and raw all along.

***

When I awaken, I'm alone. My body aches deliciously. I stretch and smile, and then I remember what brought the whole night about. How I discovered the beauty in a love that has its moments counted.

I don't want to believe it's true. What's going to happen? My mind is flooded with fear. I cover my face with my hands. I want to scream and cry; I'm so broken, and I'm not the one who's dying. I can't even begin to imagine how Peter must be feeling. I hear movement in the kitchen, so I put on my bathrobe and head in that direction.

Peter is standing in front of the sink, pouring a cup of steaming, aromatic coffee. I watch him as he reaches for the sugar, adds two teaspoons to the cup and then a trickle of milk. He's making it for me. I smile, walk over to him, and put my arms around his middle, my cheek on his back. He sets down the cup and covers my hands with his. Then he turns in my arms, facing me. I notice his overnight stubble, the faint indentation of a would-be dimple, and the restlessness in his eyes.

My heart stirs but my mind becomes angry. I want to take my fists and punch him until I'm exhausted; so instead, I hold him tighter. Why did he have to wait until he's dying to show me some affection? Why did he have to receive this diagnosis before he could hold me tenderly?

I think about the letter I have tucked into the book I am currently reading. The hope of a new life and a strong love; and I feel guilty for having allowed myself to dream. To wish.

He releases me, bringing me fully back, and gives me a delicate kiss that makes me want to hold on to him forever. I can't believe how alive I feel. I should be ashamed of this heat, but I'm not. He looks at me with a little mischief in his eyes and turns to reach for the coffee cup. As he does, my bathrobe—which wasn't very tightly closed—slides open, revealing me to him. Before I can think, I'm on the kitchen table where he kisses me with a delicately fierce urgency. I commit to memory every one of his touches, his kisses, his movements. I want to scream, cry, and laugh; but instead I pull him to me until I can feel us molding.

We are finally one.

***

"Are you hungry? Would you like some scrambled eggs?" I ask, as I put my bathrobe on, again.

"Sure," he says, pushing my hair out of my face.

He is still fantastically good-looking. Why did he have to throw us away? No! Stop it! I command myself. Don't do this to yourself. Live this. Live him.

"Why don't you sit down while I get breakfast ready?" I suggest, as I tighten my bathrobe around me and watch him pull out a chair and sit. I stare at his torso a little longer than I should and reluctantly force my eyes away from him because if I don't, breakfast won't be ready anytime soon. Wow . . . I've become a maniac for him.

I turn on the radio to drown out my erratic thoughts, and to the sweet, melodic sound of Juice Newton singing "Angel of the Morning" I go about the business of making fluffy scrambled eggs, bacon and toast.

***

I am organizing the play area at the library, willing my thoughts to straighten out as well. I've gone over our conversation in my mind time and time again, as if I can change it with replays. This time, it finally sinks in that I can't change things, no matter how much I wish upon a star.

I say his name in a whisper, and my body responds. It becomes alert, as if he was standing right here beside me. Is this how it will be when . . .? *No! Stop! Don't go there, Liana! Don't even begin thinking like that.*

I want to close my eyes and see last night and this morning all over again, but I shouldn't do so, not here. I can't remember a time when we had ever touched like that. Especially in recent years, during which our intimacy had reached an attitude of indifference. If it happened, it happened. We would go to each other because our bodies wanted to, not necessarily because our minds and souls completely agreed.

I've never stopped being physically drawn to him, especially when he walks around the house barefoot, his well-worn jeans hugging his tight waist, with an air of nonchalance evaporating from him because he doesn't know how devastatingly handsome he is.

But his heart, that place I have failed to heat with my love—that's what's destroying me. What has had me on the edge of letting go. What had me thinking that the answers lay in the heart of a different man.

However, all thoughts of leaving him evaporated last night. All images of something *new* were shattered in my mind. All I could feel was the depth of my love for him. But now, in the light of day, things aren't so clear. I don't know if his current affection will last. I don't know if he will go back to being cold and distant. I don't know what to expect, what to say or what to do. I thought my love for him was dead, but it's obviously not. Its roots are still grounded in my heart.

I guess only time will give me the answers I so desperately need. I finish the play area and head back to the counter, as I order myself not to think.

***

Nina has been very talkative today. Her wedding preparations are in full swing. Her future is open. She can't see past the engagement ring she wears and stares at, on occasion, for minutes at a time. She gushes with expectation and I dislike her for it. Life is not as beautiful as she makes it seem.

As she talks to our patrons, I half observe her. As far as looks are concerned, she's not exactly beautiful. Her eyes are so close together one would swear she's cross-eyed. Her nose is thin and points straight down. She's as thin as a broomstick. Her hair is long and blond, and she wears it with long bangs. Each one of those features alone could make her ugly, but put together on her, it works.

As far as disposition is concerned, she has an easy, open way of talking to others; she pulls them in. Almost everyone she waits on asks her about her upcoming wedding. As librarians, we're not usually in the spotlight. We're the ones alphabetizing the works written by the ones who are, but now she has her moment to be noticed, and she's enjoying it.

Finally, it's winding down time and just she and I are left, waiting for the clock to tell us it's time to lock the doors.

"Liana, can I ask you something?" she asks, twirling a strand of hair between her fingers. Her eyes dance all around me, as if she's uncomfortable with her upcoming question.

Uh-oh, I think. This sounds deep. I can't do deep right now. I have enough of that going on. But I smile and say, "Sure. What is it?"

"I was kind of hoping you could give me some advice."

I groan loudly in my mind. No. I'm not the person you need to be asking for advice, whatever kind of advice it might be. My life is a royal mess and my mind can't handle the complex choices it's faced with. I'm liable to lead you astray in whatever I say, even if by some stroke of ridiculous luck I say the right thing.

Instead of voicing my thoughts, I ask, "What kind of advice?"

"It's about the bachelorette party. Did you have one? What do girls usually do at them? Would it be better for me to do something less crazy?"

I exhale. This isn't so bad. "What makes you think a

bachelorette party is crazy?"

"Because I've seen some in the movies, and they seem kind of . . ." She pauses looking for an adequate word.

"Kind of what?"

"I don't know. Wild?"

I chuckle. "Oh, Nina. How old are you?"

"Nineteen."

I smile without cheer. "You're still young. I hate to break it to you, but not everything is like what you see in the movies." Not life, not love, not death. It's all commercialized, romanticized, and made more attractive in order for it to sell. But again, these are thoughts I don't voice.

She smiles shyly, and says, "I know that. But, they do have to get the ideas from somewhere. There must be some truth."

"You've really never been to one?"

"No," she says and blushes.

"I see. We'll I'm not an expert by any means, but you could have something small with only your closest friends. You could have finger foods, some wine and fun music. And, of course, there would be gifts."

"What about the firefighters?" she asks. "Aren't those like mandatory?"

Now, I can't help but laugh. "Girl, no. They're not mandatory at all. Girls can have fun without them, although I'm not saying that's what *you* should do."

She giggles and then picks up the speakerphone to announce the library's closing for the night.

PETER

I had to call in today, and that triggered an exhausting conversation with Joseph. I had to tell him. Honestly, he now knows more than my wife.

After setting the phone back on its cradle, I lie back down and close my eyes. However, as tired as I am, I cannot sleep. All I can do is think about how Liana looked this morning.

As she was making breakfast, I watched every one of her movements. I observed everything I've taken for granted. The gracefulness in her actions, how her calves flexed when she reached for something, how she purses her lips while she concentrates. I laugh at myself. Who would've thought making breakfast could be so sexy?

I sit up and look out the window towards the yard, and think back to the night before. When I saw the fire in her eyes, I came alive. A violent desire to live and be the man she deserves overtook me. I wanted to pull her close and make her mine with animal intensity. But I couldn't; she was making the calls, and I was willing to go at her pace. I didn't know if I would ever have another chance to love her. And, surprise! This morning I did. But how much longer will this last?

Now that I'm sitting here alone, all I can do is reflect on life, on what if's. How different I would have been had I known that I would die so young. Or maybe that's what dying people tell themselves in order to excuse some of the decisions they have made. I really can't guarantee that I would have done anything differently.

Case in point; this morning I was off in la-la land when the sound of a plate being set on the table startled me out of my thoughts. She was standing so close, I could have reached out and touched her; but instead I clenched my fists in my lap and managed a hoarse thank you. She went back to the counter, grabbed her plate and sat in the chair closest to me. We ate in silence surrounded by winter sunlight, carnal fulfillment, and a bogus peace.

About halfway through my eggs, I couldn't take another bite. I leaned back in my chair and felt that now familiar sting start in my stomach and ricochet through my chest. I must have grimaced because Liana looked at me, worry coloring her face.

"Are you okay?" she asked.

"I'm fine," I said. "I feel kind of tired. I'm going to go lie down."

I dumped my leftovers into the trashcan, put my plate and cup in the sink, and made my way to the living room. There, I stretched out on the couch, turned on the television, closed my eyes, and rode out another wave of pain.

I felt Liana come into the room. I was lying there one hand over my stomach, my other arm across my eyes. I didn't want to move. Then I felt a blanket being set over me.

"Thanks," I said, still without looking.

She touched my face with the back of her hand, and in that moment, I felt so guilty for putting her through this and fleetingly thought that I should set her free; but right on the heels of that thought, I felt selfish. I want her with me even while I'm sick. I'll be dead soon enough; then she'll be free. I can't believe I just had that thought. How morose can I be?

In an attempt to silence my mind, I turned my face slightly and kissed the back of her hand. She leaned down and kissed me lightly on the lips, and then she left.

I hear studio laughter coming from the television. I can't make out the show. Becoming irritated, I turn down the volume to where it's a low buzz and finally fall asleep.

***

My face is covered in mud. All you can see are the whites of my eyes and my teeth, if I smile. Bobby Joe and I have been splashing in mud puddles, trying to catch slippery frogs. We're having a competition to see who can catch the most. So far, I have three and he has four. The rain stopped a little while back; and you can smell the earth's quiet perfume.

"I got one!" Bobby Joe yells triumphantly.

I stomp in mock frustration. I can't let him win. So I find the messiest, smelliest, craziest hole and dive in bottom first. (That's my way of saying I slipped). After I find my bearings, I begin digging and hit gold. Four small frogs are waiting for my greedy hands to try and catch them. I make my move, and all four jump in different directions, causing me to lose my balance and Bobby Joe to erupt in laughter.

I can't be mad at him, so I do the only thing I can think of. When he's bent over laughing, I reach out and pull him in. We roll around in the mud as only two care-free boys can do.

***

I wake up smiling. I can almost feel the cool, crisp water washing over me and taking away my dirt and grime. I wonder what happened to Bobby Joe. I haven't thought of him in a long while. Once my mother died, I never sought him out again. I was so lost in my grief, the whole world around me died.

This dream reminds me that my life wasn't always

so sad or drab. That day, my mom didn't reprimand me, even though I still had dirt in my hair and ears. She just ran hot water in the shower and had me wash until all shadows of dirt were gone.

She always showered me with love, giving me quick kisses and tight hugs; even though my father told her she was turning me into a sissy. He said that she needed to be tougher with me so that I'd turn into a "real man," whatever that means. If it means to have an un-yielding, confused, somewhat inflexible heart, then I guess I did turn into one of *those*. I wish now I would've turned into the version of a man my mom was conditioning me to be.

I had my own set of chores to do, almost from the time I learned to hold a spoon. Per my father, the only thing that could keep me away from those was school and maybe a fever, depending on how high it was.

In the summertime, I'd get up early and work in the fields; and in the early evening I would find my friend Bobby Joe Thompson. He and his family were our closest neighbors, and it was perfect since we were the same age, rode the bus to school together and lived parallel lives. We loved to swim in the creek, explore in the woods behind his house, and frog hunt.

And boy, did we love to watch *Bonanza*! As soon as the theme song came on, my blood would start galloping in my veins. Lorne Greene and Pernell Roberts were my heroes, and the Ponderosa was my dream hometown. Sometimes, we would watch the show in our underwear and cowboy hats, holding toy guns at the ready to help with the bad guys.

I should ask Liana to get me a copy of the show.

Yeah . . . if you'd have seen me then, before I lost my mom, you would've thought I had it made. But it wasn't meant to be. I was meant to be broken.

***

Liana comes home from work. As she's walking in, the phone rings and, upon answering, she mouths to me that it's Daisy. I walk into the kitchen and start on dinner, listening to her occasional bursts of laughter, and relishing in its pleasant tone. When she ends her conversation, she helps me finish dinner, as we speak about her day.

As she talks, I zero in on the way her lips move, and all I want to do is pull her to me and kiss her passionately. But, I don't. Instead, I venture a light touch here and there. It's not normal for me, but she accepts and returns. Slowly, we're stoking the fizzle of last night's fire, and after dinner and waiting, we give each other a profound, less-frenzied kind of love.

***

Now, it's five o'clock in the morning and I'm wide awake. Liana sleeps soundly beside me. I reach out and cover her hand lightly, and watch her. Again I'm shaken with the realization of how lucky I am. I love waking and seeing her beside me, in the soft glow of another budding day. It's so different from the days before I met her, when I would wake up before the day did—alone.

Those days I tried not to think. I existed for the sole purpose of being. I didn't have a definite path. I wasn't concerned with love. I woke, worked and slept. I moved around from job to job until I found Mr. Saunders. He owned a dairy and didn't like conversation—he only cared that I knew how to do my job. We suited each other fine.

My first chore was to milk the cows. They were so used to their routine that they waited for me by the door. I hardly ever had to do any rounding up. The dairy was a small-sized operation. I handled most everything by myself. The cows would come in one door, where their udders were sprayed and cleaned before I'd hook them up to the milking machine.

But before I did that, I always filled one cup of fresh, creamy milk for myself. Then all the work began. Once I finished with the milking, I would clean and disinfect everything I had used. By the time I finished, the cows were out to pasture, grazing.

I kept going, all day, methodically working. I didn't

think about anything but what I was accomplishing through my hands. By the time the day was done, the second milking had been completed and I was spent.

Now I think about it and I can taste the milk and smell the cows. I can't believe I'm getting nostalgic over milking cows. But, truth be told, as hard as those days were, they were easy. The ones I'm living now are unstable, difficult and frightening.

LIANA

A poet. That's who's in love with me. I have another letter I received in my reading book, though I don't have to unfold it to know what it says. I have it committed to memory. It wasn't a lengthy letter this time. It was a poem by Thomas Ford.

> *Liana,*
> *Today I must borrow words to speak to you, for my mind fails to produce anything special. Please forgive my clumsiness and take these words by Thomas Ford as a present. A present from my heart to yours.*

> *"There is a lady sweet and kind,*
> *Was never a face so pleased my mind;*
> *I did but see her passing by,*
> *And yet I'll love her till I die.*

Her gesture, motion, and her smiles,
Her wit, her voice my heart beguiles,
Beguiles my heart, I know not why,
And yet, <u>I'll love her till I die</u>.

Cupid is winged and he doth range,
Her country, so, my love doth change.
But change she earth, or change she sky,
Yet, <u>I will love her till I die</u>."
Your admirer

I close my eyes and sigh, sure that I'm falling in love. But with whom? What face do I give this mystery man? Can I pretend it's my husband writing to me; so I can find a deep love for him, in me, or do I continue to fantasize about an imaginary being and slip further away from Peter?

It is now January; several weeks since Peter told me he's sick, and we're pretty much back to being us. The fire we shared that December night fizzled quickly. Now, I'm not insensitive; I see his decline, and I don't expect unbridled passion, where I would struggle to catch my breath from one encounter to the next. That only happens in novels or movies. All I'm asking for are a few cuddles and kisses. But, it appears those went the way of the melting snow back in December.

I don't know what to do or what to say anymore. I

don't know if he wants compassion or only my presence. I'm finding it hard to hover over him after we have both retreated into our shells. At times he's almost hurtful, as if it was my fault he was sick; especially when he's having a really hard day. On one of those days, he even accused me of just waiting for him to die so that I could find someone "not sick." I couldn't believe he could come up with an accusation like that!

And then, this letter arrives. I had managed to put the first one out of my mind. I haven't had time to think about anything but Peter's needs. Selfishness cannot be a factor in my care for him. Yet, here I am, with another dose of hope. And I'm doubly confused. I thought about not opening it; thought about laying it beside the other one in my book, but I can't stick to that idea. My heart is curious and starved for words of love. For words of hope. For words of beauty.

I'm pondering all of this as I help Peter settle in for a nap. If he could hear my thoughts, he'd be terribly disappointed. He would know my heart isn't as devoted to him as it once was. He would know that I don't really want to be here, even when I do. How it would break his heart to know that duty is what keeps me here. Or maybe that's the romantic in me thinking he would be devastated. Maybe he would be relieved. I don't even know any more.

I head to our bedroom with these tangled thoughts

clouding up my head. There, I change the bedsheets and make the bed. I pick up our discarded clothing and take everything with me to the washroom. As I sort clothes, measure detergent, and load the washer, I hear a car outside, then a closing door. I'm unsure if it's outside our house or the neighbors, but I go and check anyway, just in case.

I walk by Peter, who's sleeping soundly on the couch, and peer out the window to find Joseph walking up the driveway. He has a guitar with him and before he reaches the door, I open it.

"Liana," he says cheerily.

"Hi Joseph, come in."

As he's entering, he asks after Peter, and I nod toward his sleeping form.

"I can come back later," he starts.

I interrupt him, "No, don't. It's fine. I was about to make a cup of tea. Would you like one?"

"Sure."

In the kitchen, I fill a kettle pot with water, add tea bags to two cups, and wait for the water to boil. I look out towards Peter and am somewhat astonished at how much weight he's lost. The kettle whistles and I turn my attention back to it, trying to occupy my hands and not my mind. I add water to the cups, hand one to Joseph, and then sit across from him.

"How are you holding up?" he asks.

I shrug, not taking my eyes off my tea. I watch as the tea bag's movements make little ripples across the surface before I finally answer. "Fine, I guess."

I take out the tea bag and lay it on the plate I brought with me. I think about taking a sip, but I can't pick up the cup—I'm shaking.

"Hey, hey," he says, scooting his chair close to me and putting his hand over mine. "What is it?"

I let silent tears fall.

"Liana, do you want to talk about it?"

"It's just that . . . I don't understand. I'm to a point where I don't know what to say or how to act. I feel like I'm not doing . . . enough."

"Don't do that," he tells me softly. "There's no reason why you should be so hard on yourself. All you need to do is be there for him. We both know how crazy he is about you."

I fight hard to hold back a snicker. If only Joseph knew how cold Peter has been—and for how long. How hard it's been for us to connect. How difficult things are.

"It's hard for me too, you know. He's my best friend, and there's not a thing in the world that I can do to help him."

"Hmmm . . ." I say, and change the subject.

"Why the guitar?" I ask.

He takes his hand away from mine, and for some reason, it makes me sad.

"I was hoping to convince him to play again."

"It has been a while," I concede, wiping away my tears. "He played beautifully."

***

Without thinking, I close my eyes and I find us by the side of the lake, dripping from our swim, covered in towels. Peter, Joseph, Daisy and me.

"I'm thinking it's time to eat," Joseph said. And, together with Peter, they unload our picnic from the truck. We had sandwiches, potato salad, lemonade, and cookies.

We all finished drying off, changed into clean clothes, and passed out the food. While we ate the sun started descending. The wind was barely there and we were having a grand old time. Once it was dark, the boys gathered wood and started a fire. Across the lake, other fires glowed, their heat rising, comingling and disappearing. We were on the private side, the land owned by Joseph's family.

Soft ripples moved delicately across the water. The moon was hidden behind a puff of clouds, and crickets were trying to find a tune to their song.

Joseph untangled himself from Daisy's embrace and went to the truck only to return with Peter's Ibanez guitar. Playfully, he tossed it to him and immediately Peter began strumming. Nothing specific. Like the crickets, he was looking for a tune.

It didn't take him long to find one. I don't know much about scales or notes but I could feel the harmony. His strumming became precise, fluid, his fingers glided on the strings, effortlessly. He caressed the guitar, and in turn, it gave him its music. The notes came together, and Joseph started singing. "Hurt so Good" by John Mellencamp was the song. I closed my eyes and swayed along to the music, allowing myself to become immersed in its liveliness.

Suddenly Joseph's voice stopped; and I opened my eyes to find him and Daisy locked in a passionate kiss, her legs around his waist and her fingers locked in his hair. I looked away embarrassed but not surprised. She'd never been one for modesty. Daisy did as Daisy wanted. I looked towards Peter who had stopped playing. He was looking out into the night—lost in his thoughts.

***

I hear my name, but his lips don't move. I hear it again. I look around to see who's talking, but the images I just had, are gone. There's a touch on my shoulder.

I open my eyes and I'm no longer at the lake. I'm in my kitchen, clutching a cold cup of tea with Joseph as my witness.

I wipe my eyes with my hands.

"I'm sorry," I tell him.

"It's okay. Don't apologize," he says, his voice almost a whisper within its comfort. "I'll be honest. I've done some of that myself but don't go around telling anyone. I don't want to tarnish my reputation," he says and gives me a sad, crooked smile.

I return his smile and appreciate his attempt at humor. I really shouldn't be so gloomy; Peter's still with me. But, I'm scared and I don't know how to deal with it.

"I think he's waking up," Joseph tells me. "I'll go to him, you rest," he says.

I nod, grateful.

As he leaves my side, he reaches for the guitar.

"Hey there mate," he says. "Look what I found."

Peter's eyes lighten up and his smile softens his face. "Where'd you find that old thing?" He reaches for the guitar; and as soon as it's situated on his lap he begins to strum reverently.

Joseph glances back at me, smiles, and winks. I look away.

I need to get a meal together. But instead of thinking of what I can make, all I can concentrate on are the sounds coming from the living room—from Peter's hands. I feel like I'll suffocate from the emotions that overcome me. I have to get away. I throw my cold tea in the sink and quickly head for our bedroom.

But the sound from the guitar follows me, and doesn't let me run away.

PETER

I am genuinely happy to see my best friend. As I strum lazily, a grin blooms in my heart, and fixes on my face.

"Have you been here long?" I ask.

"Nah. I think I caught the trail end of your snoring," he responds.

I shake my head and laugh.

"So, are you going to play something?"

I shrug and look over at Liana who's moving around in the kitchen. Inspiration strikes. My fingers find the sequence to "Brown Eyed Girl" by Van Morrison.

She turns to me with tears glistening her eyes. God, she's beautiful. Why have I thrown her love away? When did I convince myself that it was okay to take our life for granted? How could I have possibly believed that it would take from my manhood? And worse yet, why don't I do anything about it?

I tried to, in the early stages of our marriage. I would spend hours mulling over what I could do to show her my love, but then when I was close to her my resolve always faltered. It felt like I was trying to wear someone else's skin, and I never gave myself the chance to settle into it. I felt like she would think I wasn't being sincere. She never said anything; it was my head that wouldn't stop telling me so, and I allowed those negative thoughts to consume me. I was weak when faced with my inner being.

She sets down the rag she's using to clean, pushes the loose hair from her face, and heads to the bedroom. I stop playing.

Joseph watches the exchange between us, and when we hear the door close he asks, "Is everything okay?"

I scoff. "As well as it can be, I suppose. We're taking things kind of hard."

He looks at me without a shred of judgement. "What can I do?"

"Nothing," I reply and change the subject, since I don't want to talk about my inadequacies with marriage. "I finally went," I say, without having to explain.

"Really? How'd that go?" he asks, settling back on the couch.

"It was okay. Heck, it was better than I'd envisioned. He's remarried and I have two half-sisters."

"Wow! How do you feel about that?

I give the question some thought, then shrug it off. "It's whatever."

"How old are they?"

"They're seven and five—Eden and Brae—and his wife's name is Vivian. They're a very good-looking bunch."

"Are you glad you went?"

"Yeah . . . I guess . . . I don't know," I say, and set the guitar beside me on the couch.

"What's he like?"

"Nice," I respond without thinking. "He seemed . . . happy." As soon as I say it out loud, I have mixed emotions. Of course it's okay that he was able to move forward and find love again, even form a new family, but how could he have gotten over my mother?

How I wish she could be with me now. I could always tell her if something frightened me, and she would hold me and make me feel safe. And, better yet, she never laughed or made me feel like it was wrong for me to have a soft side. She even used to say that I'd make someone a fine husband one day because of it. If she only knew how grandly I failed her there.

"Are you okay with that?"

I mentally rewind our conversation to figure out what he's asking me. Ah, yeah, my father being happy.

"I guess. I mean I thought it would bother me, even make me angry, but now it's fine. She seems nice, and the girls appear very well-mannered. He even has a picture of us, mom and me, on his mantelpiece. All this time I thought he had gotten rid of everything; but there we were, on display in his living room."

"So he held on to you."

"He held on to us. I just wish he would've told me, you know, instead of . . . Oh well. Can't change the past, huh?" I stand up to stretch. "You want some water?"

"Sure, thanks." He doesn't offer to get it for us. He doesn't see me as an invalid. He doesn't smother me. For that I am grateful. There will be plenty of time for hand-and-foot service, but not yet.

I return with two glasses of water and hand him one. "Does Liana know?"

"I haven't told her yet, but they want to meet her."

We drink from our glasses, contemplating, and then I hear her coming towards us. She's changed into a pair of jeans and a pomegranate-pink pullover sweater. Her eyes are a little puffy, and I wish I could be granted the power to take away all her pain.

"I'm headed to the grocery store. You guys want anything?"

"No, thanks," I reply.

"Okay then. I won't be long."

She walks to the door, takes her jacket off the hook, puts it on, grabs her purse and walks out the door. I've never been so intent in watching her, but now I take in everything about her, every one of her movements, facial expressions—especially when she doesn't know I'm watching. I'm committing it all to memory. I'm taking her with me, when I go.

***

I sit back down, feeling somewhat tired. I reach for the remote and turn on the TV, searching until I find the game. We watch as the Cowboys battle against the Giants, who are on their way to securing their spot at the Super Bowl next month. I don't really care who wins; it's something to watch, or better yet, background noise for the current of my thoughts.

I watch the series of rushes, fumbles, and touchdowns, all the while thinking of what I must do. What I need to ask of my friend.

Cutting into my thoughts, Joseph says, "I think it's a good idea for them to meet."

"I was thinking the same thing." The announcer interrupts me with the narration of Emmitt Smith's touchdown. He sounds so excited, I let him finish; then I go back to our conversation. "I just don't know how to bring him up, especially since I've never welcomed any conversations about him."

"I'm positive you won't have a problem telling her. She'll understand. Would you want them to come here, or would you take her there?"

"I'd rather go there, since he's still in my childhood

home. I'd like for her to see it."

"That sounds nice."

A break for commercials and I make up my mind. I look at him directly and say, "Listen, Joseph, there's something I have to ask you."

He leans forward, and gives me his undivided attention. "What is it?"

"It's something quite big and I hope that you'll agree to do this for me."

"Consider it done."

"But I haven't told you what it is."

"You will, and I'll do it," he responds immediately.

I take a deep breath, exhale, and ask him for the favor of a lifetime.

LIANA

I close the door behind me. The cold winter air assaults me, but I feel like I can finally breathe. I fill my lungs until they feel like they're on the verge of freezing, then I sit in my car. After a short warm-up, I back out and proceed to the store.

Peter's face comes to me as I drive, but I don't want to think. Matter of fact, I left the house so I could stop thinking. So, I turn on the radio. Elvin Bishop's voice reaches me with "Fooled Around and Fell in Love." I can't do it. I press the Scan button on the radio, searching for the next available station; and hear:

"Heaven help us, baby's got her blue jeans on.
She can't help it if she's made that way,
She's not to blame if they look her way . . ."

This I can work with. My previous thoughts are blurred; relegated to the back of my mind. I have no idea who's singing—until the DJ says it's Mel McDaniel with "Baby's Got Her Blue Jeans On." I'm tapping the steering wheel as I pull into the grocery store parking lot. I feel a whole lot better.

As soon as the doors slide open, the heat coming from the vents slams my face. I pick up my pace, grab a cart, and head for the meat department where I select a rotisserie chicken for the chicken wild rice soup I decided I'm going to make for dinner.

Santana and Rob Thomas's "Smooth" follows me from aisle to aisle as I select veggies, pasta, and a few peaches for a cobbler. The music changes, as I'm checking out, to a pop song. I hear, "I'm a genie in a bottle, baby," and I grimace wondering what happened to the real music, the real lyrics, the stuff that makes you *feel*. Thankfully, I'm all checked out and heading out the door as the next singer is telling the world that, "Oops, I did it again."

***

As I drive down our street, I see the mail truck rounding the corner to the next street. My heart rate accelerates, as does the speed of the car. Did he deliver another letter? Did Peter bring in the mail? Am I fretting over nothing? What would he do? What would he say if he discovered the letters?

I can't have them taken from me.

Some might not understand, might even think me cold in keeping the letters while my husband withers away. To them, I don't want to apologize. I will not even attempt an explanation because to their ears it will not make sense. And I'm okay with their judgments as long as I keep receiving the letters that allow me to hope, to believe, to long.

I nearly run to my front door, struggling to keep a good grip on the plastic grocery bags I'm carrying, and reach into the mailbox. The mail is still there. I exhale relieved.

Walking in, I set the groceries down on the table; then I go through the mail. There, in between the weekly circulars, is my lilac envelope. I hold it to my breast and close my eyes, my head now dizzy with yearning.

A closing door takes me away from the moment, and I hurry to secure the envelope inside my purse. I then begin unloading the groceries, willing my hands to stop trembling and count to stabilize my breath.

Joseph walks in from the hallway. "Need help?"

I venture a wistful peek towards my purse; but duty calls and dinner must be served, so I pull my heart from my wish to dream and settle it on reality.

"Sure, thanks. You can shred this," I say as I open the package of rotisserie chicken. "Is Peter asleep?"

"Yeah, he took his medicine and knocked out," he replies washing his hands. He clears his throat several times.

"Is everything okay?" I ask.

"Yeah, it's just that . . ." Another throat-clearing. "I have some news."

"Oh, really? What is it?"

"I uh . . . I met someone," he says as he tackles the chicken, shredding it.

My heart shivers slightly, and I frown into the pot that's swimming with chicken broth, wild rice, sage, thyme, salt and pepper. I don't feel happy for him, and I don't know why. I quickly practice a smile and turn to him; he seems so shy, so unlike him.

"That's great!" I utter. He stays quiet. "What is it?" I ask. "Aren't you excited?"

"Yes, of course I am. It's just that I feel kind of guilty, you know? With Peter . . ." He trails off and looks away from me.

I reach for his arm. "I know. But don't feel bad. You're not doing anything wrong."

"But, it's like, how can I do this? How can I think of a future, when he's planning an end?"

"Don't!" I say emphatically. And in a softer voice I add, "I know what you mean. Seeing something like this, living it, it's tough and unfair, but . . ."

"It makes you want to live, to cherish life while you

have it," he says, finishing for me.

I look away, sad for having those exact thoughts, and elated because someone understands.

"Does this make us horrible people?" I ask.

"Nah, I think it only makes us human," he responds, reaching for me in an awkward hug since his hands are still covered in the aftermath of his work with the chicken. There, in each other's arms, we allow ourselves the chance to think of the future.

I end the embrace, a little unnerved by how I enjoyed his solidity. "So who is she?"

He smiles and heads for the sink. "Her name is Juliet."

"Oh, so now you're Romeo?" I tease.

He laughs, "Hardly. Not even close."

"When can we meet her?"

"I'm not sure. I kind of want to let it go a little further, you know?"

I nod. "I'm happy for you. I know it's been a while."

"It sure has," he sighs, and runs his hands through his hair.

Neither one of us mention Daisy, although it's evident she's on both our minds, along with the pain she inflicted with her departure.

"Well, whenever you're ready, let me know. I'll cook a special dinner."

"That would be perfect," he says. "She needs to meet my two favorite people." He winks and hands me the chicken, which I add to my simmering pot.

***

Peter is fast asleep and I know he won't be waking any-time soon. The medicine knocks him out for the night. I've finished cleaning up after dinner, and now I am finally alone with my letter. I am again taking my time, torturing myself with the desire to know what new thoughts have sprung from my admirer's mind. From the mind of the man who makes me feel important and beautiful and loved.

I tuck my legs under me and open the envelope. A faint smell of him glides toward me. It's a smell that I've never noticed before and one that I now look for everywhere I go. I can't even describe it. All I can say is it's a very masculine, clean, soft, rainy-day, sexy type of scent. It makes me think of someone polished, se-cure, tall, and muscular, with messy hair and penetrat-ing eyes. Maybe if I can find a person who smells like this, I can figure out his identity. Solve my mystery. But so far, I've had no luck.

With my mind conjuring sculpted male physiques, with dazzling smiles, and intoxicating scents; I begin to read.

Liana,

I know I'm being selfish, somewhat cocky and maybe even pretentious in assuming that your heart has picked up a beat, that your breathing has become a little labored, and that your hands trembled just slightly since you saw my letter.

I want to assume that you're excited to read my words. All I've done lately is think about you and how wonderful you look in blue. I am going out of my mind with the desire to be near you, to touch you.

Long into the night, I think of you. I wonder how your day went and if you thought of me. I convince myself that you have, and I smile myself silly. I turn to the pillow beside me and I talk to it, sing to it, and read to it as if it were you.

You're always easy to talk to, especially on rainy days, which we've had several of late. The rain causes my melancholia to surface and makes me wish you were here—even more strongly. On those days, I've almost revealed myself, but something or other gets in the way and stops me.

I don't know how much longer I can live like this. I want to know your thoughts, to hear your words. If I were to give you an address, would you write me? Do you want to change things? I don't even know myself.

No, I won't force you to make that choice. For now, this is getting me by. I know, now I'm selfish, thinking of me. But, I also think of you. If you wrote me back, would it make you feel guilty? Would we become brazen and act on the urge to meet?

*I couldn't ask you to do anything that could jeopardize
what you have or who you are. But here I am doing just that!
How conflicting my emotions are . . . and I aspire to assume
that yours are too. I am sorry but I must tell you—because I
can hold it in no longer—that I fear I am deeply, irrefutably
in love with you. Know that you will always have my heart.*

With unmovable love,

Your admirer

I read the words over and over until the letters start
swimming before my eyes. I reach for my book—"A
Lonely Heart up for Grabs"—that I use as a hiding
place, and I tuck this letter in along with the other two.
All the while, I ask myself; would I want the ability to
write him back? Could I handle that right now? No, I
don't think I could, but I want to. Boy, do I want to!

He is right, though. I do think of him all the time.
Even while I'm caring for Peter, I think of him. I wonder, if it were him—my Secret Admirer—that I was
caring for, what would he do? What would he say?
Would he hold on to me for dear life? Would he confide
his feelings and fears to me? Would he touch my cheek
each day as he looked into my eyes as if it were the last
time he'd be able to do so? And finally, would he say I
love you over and over to me until he was convinced
that I believed him?

How I wish Peter would do all of this.

The phone rings, and I see Daisy's number on the caller id. I don't want to talk to anyone so I lower the volume, and continue sitting in my barrel of self-pity.

For another half-hour I ruminate through my conflicting thoughts. I question what love is; why we are so desperate to find it, and if it's always supposed to bring heartache with it. I compare my reality to what I thought my life was supposed to look like. I examine my heart's reactions to every situation I'm facing. I can't make sense of any of it. I groan frustrated.

And with these thought fogging up my brain, I head for bed, sure that I won't sleep well again tonight.

PETER

I'm standing in front of the mirror, scrutinizing my reflection. My skin is barely holding on to my bones. My head is shaved and my overall appearance is sallow. I look at my chest. The nasty culprit of my downfall is sitting right there, in a place where it doesn't belong. Where it's uncommon for a man. In my breast. Yes, I have breast cancer and I'm ashamed to talk about it.

The only reason I went to the doctor was because, one day, while I was in the shower I ran the bar of soap over my left pectoral and noticed a lump. I kept washing wondering why it was there and why it was a little sore to the touch. Once out of the shower, I looked at it in the mirror and noticed that my nipple was a little red. My other nipple was pink, without a lump.

I turned one way and then the other, comparing. Then I put on a t-shirt and didn't think about it until a few weeks later, again in the shower. I noticed that my nipple was folding in on itself and the lump was a little more painful. I made the decision to go to the doctor.

And now here I am with a diagnosis of breast cancer, and I can't talk openly about it because I'll be an anomaly. As much as I hate for women to get this, it's not supposed to happen to men.

Slowly I turn from my reflection and begin to dress. Today Liana and I are going to my father's house. Joseph was right. Liana didn't say anything negative about me not talking about him before.

Out in the car, I struggle to put on my seatbelt. I hadn't realized before the amount of strength it takes to pull the belt and push the end into the buckle until it clicks. I must admit that my strength is failing me. This thought is so depressing.

I give her directions on how to get there, and about fifteen minutes later as we pull into the drive, my father meets us at the car. He reaches for me, and I don't protest. It's nice to feel his touch versus his fists. I have to remind myself; that was long ago and we're no longer on that road, even if I can feel the scars burned into my heart. I have chosen to forgive, to embrace.

Once inside, I sit and introduce Liana. Vivian hugs her with all the Southern hospitality she possesses. The girls are shy at first, but once they warm up, their sweetness takes over. They show her artwork they've been working on and school awards.

I point to the picture of Mother and me on the mantel, and Vivian brings it over so that Liana can get a closer look. She's seen the one photograph I carry in my wallet, but Mother's personality really shines through in this picture. She was so young, staring at the camera with her arms around me and her chin on my shoulder. Her dress had been blown slightly to her right by the wind that picked it up at the moment the camera clicked. We're both smiling wide, honest, happy smiles. My throat clogs with emotion at the sight of her.

My father's sister took the picture. Her given name was Raina but her hippie name was Cosmic River. She wore flower crowns and tie-dyed shirts with long, flowing skirts that reached the soles of her strappy sandals. She was a free spirit who would occasionally grace us with her presence. I realize I haven't heard about her in years. I wonder where she is, what she's doing.

"Whatever happened to Aunt Raina?" I ask my father.

"Who knows. Haven't heard from her since your mom passed," he replies. "She took off with that one guy, the one who drove the lime-green van."

"Oh yeah, I remember him," I say and shiver, not from my memories, necessarily. I'm cold. So, so cold. Vivian picks up on this and immediately produces a blanket. It's a body-length fleece blanket decorated with a scene of wolves in a snowy forest, their fur blending in with the snow and their eyes shiny and attentive. It's heavy, and I'm immediately enveloped in its warmth.

My father is sitting in his recliner, looking from me to his daughters almost as if he can't believe we're all sitting here—together.

I cover up to my chin and we talk; trying to get to know each other's pasts, presents, and futures in one afternoon.

***

I must have dozed off, because the next thing I know, Liana's hand is touching my leg and she's calling my name into my ear.

"Peter, Peter."

I stir and lazily open my eyes.

"Vivian says dinner is ready," she tells me.

"How long have I been sleeping?" I ask her.

"Oh, maybe about thirty minutes."

I lay my head back, and exhale slowly.

"I can't believe I did that."

"Don't worry about," she replies, taking my hand. "Come on."

I'm not in the least bit hungry, but I slowly follow her into the dining room. I look at everyone sitting at the table, their eyes all on us, and I'm deeply grateful we came.

LIANA

A few days after we visited Peter's father; I'm cleaning up in the living room, when I hear a chipper knock at the door, which startles me. At the same time, Peter, who's been sleeping on the couch, begins coughing, so I go to him instead. His coughing turns to retching as the knocking continues.

"Come in," I yell. When I look up, my lifelong friend—Daisy—stands there, dressed in happiness. Bright-orange pants, a brilliant-white sweater, and a banana-yellow scarf. Her hair has been styled with big roller curls.

Her rich, red mouth falls open as she stares at me. She watches as Peter vomits into a trashcan while I hold him in a semi-sitting position. When there's nothing left, I lay him back down and wipe his mouth with a cloth. He doesn't even ask who was at the door, just closes his eyes.

I stand then, and motion Daisy toward the kitchen, where I can wash my hands. Before I walk away, I cover my husband's shivering body with a couple of blankets. Satisfied, I turn and follow her.

"What is going on?" she whispers, bewildered.

I shake my head while washing my hands.

"Tea or coffee?" I ask.

"Tea, but . . ."

I turn my back to her and fill a kettle with water. After setting it on the burner, I pull my ponytail tighter and finally turn to face her. Her eyes are still large with surprise and full of questions. Some of which I know I don't want to answer.

"He's sick," I say. "Cancer."

I can see more questions flitting across her face, but she's decent enough not to ask them. Instead we sit there in silence until the kettle hollers that it's finished.

Daisy stands saying, "Don't get up. I'll do it."

I'm so grateful I want to cry. My eyes fill, but I don't let them empty. I just sit there numb and tired. She sets a steaming cup in front of me and puts her arms around my shoulders, her chin on my head. That's when I let my tears fall. I put my hand on her arm and relish in the love I feel from her.

Finally, she releases me and sits in the chair closest to me. We take cautious sips from our cups—I frown when I realize she forgot to add sugar.

"How long?" she asks.

I'm not sure if she means how long he's been sick or how much longer he has, so I explain, "We found out in December. It was already too advanced for surgery. He was given three to six months." I say this like I'm reciting my grocery list.

"But, it's February now. Why didn't you call me? I would've come," she tells me, and I half smile.

"I know you would've. But, I didn't want to you to worry. Plus, you had just left for Puerto Vallarta with Danny. I didn't want to ruin your trip."

"Oh, Liana. I'm so sorry I haven't been here for you . . . but I'm here now. Tell me what you need me to do."

I can't imagine a thing she could do. She's never been good at anything domestic, since she's always had service people cooking and cleaning for her.

One time, when we were about fourteen, she tried to bake cookies to help me feel better. I'd missed school, for two days straight, with a stomach virus and she decided she'd had enough. She had free reign in our house, so she took up residence in our kitchen that afternoon. Mother was out shopping and Father was still at work.

She worked and worked, until she finally went into the living room announcing she had just placed a batch of cookies in the oven. My eyes had gone wide in surprise; I'd never known her to bake, but I thanked her.

She then proceeded to brush my hair and paint my toenails. As she did, we talked about what I'd missed at school. About how Clara was no longer Jimmy's girlfriend, because she now liked Tommy. Then, she told me Mrs. Strober, our Math teacher, had given them a surprise quiz, early in the morning, and everyone had failed.

"Do you smell that?" I asked, interrupting her monologue.

"What?" she replied, nonchalantly.

"It smells like something's burning."

"I don't smell anything."

And then, we both remembered, "The cookies!"

She dashed to the kitchen and I followed, a little slower. There was smoke coming from the oven door, and I registered the mess she'd left on the counter with the flour.

"Don't open the door," I shouted to her, as she reached for it.

"What do I do?" she asked, turning back to me, tears in her eyes.

"Just . . . turn it off."

The smoke tickled our noses and our throats—as we went about opening the windows and doors—causing us to cough uncontrollably.

"Come on," I coughed. "Let's go outside."

Once we were seated on the porch, she put her arm around me.

"I'm sorry," she apologized. "I only wanted to help you feel better."

"You did," I said, laying my head on her shoulder.

We let the house air out for about an hour, and then we went in to clean up. When we finally pulled the cookie sheet out of the oven, we dissolved in laughter. All that was left was cookie ashes.

"Next time, I'll just buy you some cookies. How's that?"

"I think that's a mighty fine idea," I replied, tossing the whole cookie sheet in the trash.

***

I look at her sitting across from me now, and suggest smiling, "How about some cookies?"

"You still remember that?" she asks laughing.

"How could I forget? You almost burnt our house down."

"It wasn't that bad."

I look at her pointedly and we giggle some more.

"Okay, yes it was. I'm surprised your mother didn't ban me from your home after that."

"She wanted to . . . I had to talk her out of it."

Sobering, she adds, "So . . . aside from cookies. What can I do?"

The fact that she's here is enough for me. And I tell her so.

"You're the best, you know."

"So I've been told," she replies, a mischievous air in her words and a wiggle to her eyebrows. I giggle, grateful for her friendship.

Images of those tender years flood my memory; especially the days when we would laugh until we cried, dancing around in my room with huge rollers in our hair and makeup cases set up all over my dresser. We would dress up in tights and crop shirts and sing our hearts out to ABBA, especially "Dancing Queen." And other times, we would talk about our crushes on George Michael as we danced to "Wake Me Up Before You Go-Go."

All of that feels like a lifetime ago, or like I'm thinking of someone else's memories.

I stand to hug her again and in that instant, I remember Joseph's coming over. I let her know.

"Oh," she hiccups in reply. A little twitch of her hands and a slight widening of her eyes are the only indicators that she's become somewhat uncomfortable. "So, he decided to stay here. In Skedaddle."

I can tell it's more a statement than a question, so I stay quiet. I'm not exactly sure how things have been between them since their divorce, three years ago. But I do know that her inability to sleep in one bed—theirs—caused their separation.

"I haven't seen him in forever," she says, and I let the conversation hang.

We sit down and enjoy a companionable silence, drinking our un-sweetened tea and mentally going our separate ways until a car in the drive reminds me of the time and that Joseph is here. Daisy didn't make a move to leave since I told her, so now there's no avoiding their encounter.

I stand and open the door to let him in. He's standing on the porch holding a big pot. I try to see him through Daisy's eyes. He is very handsome, and with age, he's settled in to his good looks. He's tall, muscular, and lean, with a heart-shaped face, a trimmed beard, and penetrating dark-brown eyes. A gray hair here and there gives a hint of maturity to his attractiveness.

"Hey," I say before, I go on analyzing him.

"Hey. Whose car is that?" he asks, signaling with a jerk of his head.

"Daisy's," I reply quietly.

"Oh." He looks inside and there, standing in his line of sight is Daisy; beautiful, tan, and gawking at him with such longing that I have to look away.

He clears his throat and shakes his head. "Right. Okay. I'll just set this down and go for the rest."

He walks past her to the kitchen and sets the pot

on the stove. He doesn't turn around right away, so she talks to his back.

"Hi Joseph," she says in a whisper.

I am a spectator of something so very intimate; I feel like an intruder.

"Joseph, is the car unlocked? I can get the rest," I say.

"No, no, it's okay. I'll do it," he quickly tells me. As he passes me, he whispers, "Do you have anything strong to go with that chili?"

I give his arm a little squeeze, and out the door he goes.

When I turn towards Daisy, she's breathing slowly and a few tears have pooled in her eyes.

"That went well," she says. "Why didn't you tell me he was coming and that he's still so good-looking?"

"I did tell you he was coming." I check to make sure he's not within hearing distance. "As for the good-looking, I hadn't noticed."

"It doesn't matter," she says.

"He comes over often to help with Peter."

"That makes sense. Best friends and all. Plus, Joseph has always been kind, caring, and helpful."

We hear him walking back up the front steps.

"I'll be right back," she says and almost runs to the bathroom.

When Joseph comes back in, I feel like I need to apologize to him. I can see how affected he is from seeing her; his breathing is somewhat angry, and his jaw is clenching.

"I'm sorry, Joseph," I say. "I didn't know she was coming."

"It's okay," he says with a dash of resentment. "It was bound to happen sooner or later. I'll be fine. Here's your mail; I picked it up on the way in. Hope you don't mind."

"Thanks." I reach for it and feel my stomach flutter as soon as I see the lilac envelope and familiar writing. As Joseph heads for the kitchen, I hide the letter between the other envelopes; hug the pile of mail to me and follow Joseph to the kitchen, where I shove everything into the drawer I keep for bills. Reading it will have to wait until later, when I'm alone.

***

When Daisy returns, she looks refreshed, like nothing out of the ordinary had taken place. Like her heart hadn't skipped several beats from the sight of Joseph. Like she hadn't eaten him up with her eyes.

"I think I'm going to go," she says, heading for her purse.

I set some bowls on the table as they talk around me and their feelings.

"You don't have to leave," Joseph says, opening the

refrigerator and pulling out a beer. "There's plenty of food here for all of us. It'll be just like old times."

But it isn't, and it can't be. Peter is sick, Joseph and Daisy are no longer a pair, and I can't wait for them to leave so that I can devour a letter from someone I don't know. Definitely, not like old times.

"If you're sure," Daisy replies hesitantly, and bites her lower lip.

"Of course, I'm sure," he says calmly, taking a drink from his beer before adding, "Why wouldn't I be?"

I look from one to the other; they appear to be locked in a stare-down, and the expressions on their faces say they want to slap each other until they draw blood and then jump into bed afterwards. There's a stern determination, an I will-not-back-down attitude, and a sexual turbulence emanating from both of them; it fills the room. I glance away from all the passionate emotions I'm witnessing.

Piercing through this crazy, sensitive encounter comes Peter's voice:

"Liana?"

"Yes, Peter."

"Can I have some water please?"

"Sure. Just a second." I go to the sink and fill a glass.

"I'll take it," Joseph says, setting his beer on the counter.

I hand him the glass and my fingers graze his—like

they've done many times before—but today they're charged, and I feel a current awaken in me.

I turn away and reach for the bowls I'd set out earlier. I observe Daisy, who hasn't finished oogling Joseph; especially now that she's getting a view of his back-side. Derriere galore.

I want to take her eyes off of him, and I do so by asking her if she'll help me set the table.

"Hello there, mate," Joseph says.

Peter opens his eyes and smiles. "Hey, what are you doing here?" he asks as if it's un-common for his friend to be at our house. As if he hadn't just seen him a couple of days ago.

"I brought you some of your favorite chili, which only I can make, and was going to see if you were up to losing a few games of dominoes."

Peter laughs. My heart tightens. Not much can make either of us laugh anymore, especially not Peter, but Joseph still has the touch. I watch as he helps Peter into a sitting position and hands him the water. Peter takes a few ginger sips and holds the glass on his lap.

"Chili huh? With cornbread?"

"Of course. No jalapeños." We all know Peter's stomach can't handle spicy foods any longer. "So what do you say? Up for some?"

Peter smiles fondly at his best friend and says, "You bet I am."

"Good. I'll go get you a bowl, and I'll eat here with you."

"Thanks." Peter glances toward the kitchen and notices Daisy for the first time. His eyes go wide and his lips open in a silent O.

"Hi, Daisy," he says, as he's turning to look at Joseph, who only shrugs and walks to the kitchen. "When did you get here?"

"Earlier today," she says walking toward him. "I just found out. I'm so sorry."

Peter waves her words away. "Not your fault. Are you staying around?" I know he's asking more for Joseph's sake than his own.

"I am now. Liana needs me," she says. But when she looks back, it's not me her eyes are searching for. It's Joseph; who has his back to her, and is busy plating food for him and Peter.

Once he's done, he carries the bowls to the living room and sits across from Peter. Daisy joins me at the kitchen table. We eat in crackling silence.

PETER

Back in the bedroom, I can't hold my tongue any longer.

"What's Daisy doing here?" I ask as Joseph lowers me onto the bed.

"I don't know. She was here when I got here."

I eye him, knowing how crazy he was about her, and I can't seem to figure out what he's thinking.

"She's still beautiful," I say.

He sighs, "Yes. Yes she is. Tan, glowing, and beautiful."

"Are you going to talk to her while she's here?"

He turns and begins rummaging through my pajama drawer, picking out my favorite gray plaid pants and an old t-shirt.

"This okay?" he asks, showing me his selections and avoiding my gaze.

I can tell he doesn't want to answer and I'm not

going to push him, but then he says, "No, I don't think I will. I mean, there's nothing left to say. She said plenty when she left."

I nod and slowly make my way to the bathroom, Joseph on my heels in case I need him but not pressing. When we're done, and I'm all clean and in bed he says, "Remember when all four of us went on vacation?"

I look at him; he's so torn. My heart goes out to him. This man is a one woman man, and the one he chose didn't know how to appreciate or value the gem she had. I guess I have no choice but to go down memory lane with him.

"Oh, do I. We had tons of fun."

"I didn't think we were ever going to convince them to go skiing."

"I know. Daisy wasn't that hard to convince, but Liana . . ."

I can still see Liana's face turned towards the sky, her cheeks colored with cold and the wind messing with her hair. An anxious smile and new-found determination were set on her face. Her eyes were wide with anticipation. Her body was bundled in winter clothes and finished off with skiing gear. She turned to look at me, and I smiled.

"Not like going to the beach, huh?" I said.

"Nope," she replied.

Our guide gave us the instructions we needed to have

a fairly safe descent. We mounted the lift that would take us to the point where we'd start. Once there, I set and pushed off. I felt like I was flying. Faster and faster I went with my gaze channeled directly ahead of me. A white, flurried world surrounded and whipped past me. I stretched my arms wide as I neared the bottom, and allowed myself the freedom of the moment.

***

Liana walks in carrying a bundle of folded laundry. No one says anything as she begins to put the clothes away in various dresser drawers. When she's done, she turns around to face us and I notice the worry lines on her face and how her shoulders seem to droop. She's tired, all because she's been taking care of me.

"I guess I'm off, too," says Joseph.

"We didn't get to play dominoes," I remind him.

"It's okay," he replies. "I'll be back tomorrow."

Liana walks him to the door and puts her hand on his arm. I can tell she's attempting to offer an apology for Daisy's presence, but there's something else too. A nagging thought begins to creep into my mind. I observe as he looks at her for a moment, then turns and leaves. I order my mind to quieten, but something was there.

"Poor guy," she says. "Looks like he still loves her."

"That's what it looks like," I agree, watching her

keenly. I need to distract my thoughts. I'm not exactly sure where they're going, or that I can stomach where they're going.

"What is she doing here, anyway?" I ask, not really caring for the answer.

"She *is* my friend," Liana tells me a little annoyed. Then, softening her voice, she adds, "She and Danny just came back from their vacation, although we didn't really talk about it. She probably came to town to see her parents."

"She finally remembered where they live?"

Liana gives me a you-better-watch-it look, even though she knows I'm not saying anything that isn't true, and walks into the bathroom.

"Is she staying long?" I ask.

"I don't know. She didn't say much once she saw Joseph." She comes back carrying the hamper and sets it by the door.

"I wonder what David would make of that?"

"Danny," Liana corrects me. "His name is Danny."

"I don't know how you keep them straight. Anyway, I take it he didn't come with her?"

"No. He went back to work."

"Well, I hope she doesn't give Joseph any trouble while she's here," I say.

"I don't think she will," she replies, reaching for the comforter and pulling it over me.

I've already taken my pain medication so, with my pain somewhat under control, I lie back. As soon as her hand is close to my face, I grab it. She doesn't pull away.

"Thank you," I say. "For everything."

"Don't say it," she whispers. "It's not necessary."

"You have no idea how I wish things were different. You deserve so much more than this."

"Peter. Stop."

I'm still holding on to her hand, so she sits beside me. I look directly into her eyes and say, "Promise me that you'll be happy when . . ." I can't finish.

She gasps and pulls her hand away from me, putting it to her neck, almost as if I had hit her there. We know it's coming, but we haven't talked about it. We just don't want to face it. It's like, if we say it, it becomes real. (Not that it's fake otherwise).

"Peter, I . . . I can't."

"But, I need you to."

"Why?" She doesn't face me; she fidgets with the comforter instead.

"Because I need to know that you'll be okay. That you'll find someone who deserves you. That you'll be happy." I pause briefly, then add, my voice faltering, "As happy as I failed to make you."

I cringe at the thought of her with another man, at the thought of that man touching her, seeing her, loving her. At the thought of her hands touching another man's skin the way she has touched me . . . and I am sick with jealousy. But I have to put it in check; as hard as it is for me, I know it has to be. I can't expect her to pine for me all her life. She's still young. She could even have kids. Oh my Lord! I groan frustrated; this isn't the first time I've had these thoughts, and I really must stop torturing myself.

All I wanted was to make her happy, and now someone else will get to do that; and I have to be okay with it. I fist my hands weakly.

She walks to the window, staring out to the darkness. "Liana?"

"Not now, Peter," she says, turning back to me. "We can talk about it later. There's still time."

Not much, I think, but I don't say it.

She heads for the door.

"Are you not going to sleep?" I ask.

"I'm going to finish cleaning up," she says, turning out the lights and picking up the hamper. "I'll be back."

With that, she leaves me in the dark with my torturous thoughts and the pain, which is faintly making itself known. I close my eyes and see Joseph standing at the door with Liana's hand on his arm, and my imagination takes off. Visions of them together float through my mind, and I sigh angrily. The meds need to kick in so I won't think. So I won't feel.

LIANA

I cannot get away from the bedroom fast enough. I can't believe the way this day has ended. And Peter trying to make me promise. I couldn't look at him. It's not that I want him to die, but I know it's going to happen . . . and it could be the guilt I feel that makes me so uneasy. Guilt from already having someone who gives me something to look forward to.

I'm trembling violently. I must calm down. I head to the kitchen to find my letter. I'm like an addict; feverish and choleric while searching for their vice. As soon as I see mine, I feel my body reacting—relaxing. I feel hope, which comes from knowing that whatever words I find, they'll make me feel better.

Carefully, I pick up my letter and carry it to my favorite chair in the patio. And there, I am finally alone. With him.

Liana,
I had a thought of you today, and this is what it turned to:

A beautiful song was written,
And birds were summoned to carry its tune.
Flowers were given their colors,
To brighten the smile that's in you.
I find your face in the formations,
Of the stars that I see through the night.
And I sense your sweet caresses,
In the winds that pass me by.
How I wish I could stand before you,
And tell you how I feel.
But there is no courage in a coward,
Who walks alone in fear.

A coward, Liana. That's what I am. I try to convince myself otherwise, but I cannot. I've been close enough to touch you, on more than one occasion, and I make myself walk away. I let my hand fall before it rises in your direction. I inhale your scent as you walk by and I carry it with me. I walk away, not because I am strong, but because I am a coward.

You, on the other hand, are brave. Immensely so. I imagine it is not easy to love someone who is dying. I could not do what you do. You are an example to me. A hero.

Your heart is delicate and invaluably strong. Your smile, though now it wavers, is absolutely divine. I hope I have made it through your mind today and have stolen at least a couple hundred of those smiles, as you have mine.

Sleep well, my dear. Dream of hope. Dream of future. Dream of love.

Your Admirer

I close my eyes and hold this new letter to my beating heart. I allow myself to dream; to smile. But how can I grant my heart this reprieve?

I think about the promise Peter asked me to make. It must've broken his heart to utter those words, yet he had done so. How strong he must be, and what a fraud I am. I curl into my distress and cry bitter tears. Some are for me, others are for Peter, for Joseph, for Daisy, for my letter writer, for everyone who has known a love and lost it, for everyone who has watched a loved one die, for everyone who has had to bury their dreams and live with a hole in their heart.

Looking for comfort, I let my eyes rest on the words before me . . .

I imagine it is not easy to love someone who is dying.

I sit up shocked. How does he know about Peter? Who have I talked to about him? I read it again. I go through my mind. Who? No one materializes in my head. I have to let the thought fade for now, and continue reading.

I could not do what you do. You are an example to me. A hero.

I shake my head sadly. I'm not a hero. I'm not strong. A hero doesn't hide behind a curtain of fear. A hero fights until the end; even when their opponent is much bigger.

I am only a woman who is lost. A woman who loves and wishes to be loved in return. A woman who is trying to live the life she's been given and wishing it wasn't at all what it is. A woman who stays where she's needed while her heart walks away.

***

The next day, as I'm manning the reception desk, a woman walks in with a small flower arrangement.

"Liana Hartsfield?" she asks.

"That's me."

"These are for you," she says, handing me the small pot full of pink roses and white daisies.

"Thank you," I reply, and immediately look for the card. I open it and all it says is:

Thinking of you,
Your Admirer.

I smile, thankful for the gesture and in the same thought I wonder why it never occurred to Peter that something like this, something so small, could be so meaningful. I take in the smell of the flowers and think I need to get back to work, as much as I would love to just stand here and daydream.

"How's Peter doing?" Marjorie asks me as I take books from the drop-off box.

"Not well," I tell her.

"I'm so sorry, honey," she says with a slow shake of her head.

I don't respond. I can't say it's okay, because it's not. And I can't say that it isn't her fault or that there's nothing she can do because it's obvious and unnecessary.

"What have the doctors said?"

"Not much. It's all a matter of managing the pain; of helping him find comfort in his final days. Everything is moving so quickly, and yet it feels like it's happening in slow motion."

I wait for her to check-out a patron. Then she turns back to me and asks, "What do you need? How can I help?"

I halfway shrug. "There's really nothing. Joseph's been staying with him while I work, but I think I'm going to have to find a nurse or if it gets worse . . ."

"Hospice?"

I nod.

"You really think it's time?"

"It's very close," I say tearing up. And who's standing in line right as I reach for a Kleenex? Malcolm.

"Are you okay?" he asks, without a hint of his previous flirtation.

I wipe my eyes quickly, "Yes, I'm fine, thanks. Are you ready to check out?"

"Yes, please." He sets his books down, and hands me his library card. This time when my fingers brush his, I feel nothing.

"Those flowers are beautiful," he remarks.

"Thanks," I say as I scan his books, thinking to the last time I saw him, how he had affected me. Today I'm un-concerned with his presence. His dimpled smile doesn't make me falter, and his eyes don't make me want to get lost in them. If he were my writer, I think, I would *feel* it.

I wish him happy reading, and with a small pause, he makes his way out the door.

***

About an hour later, Daisy arrives to take me to lunch. Since I'm downtown, we walk a couple of blocks to Andy and Sandy's. We choose a table by the window and order the soup of the day with salads.

"I spoke with Danny earlier. I told him I'm staying

here a bit longer," she says.

"How'd he take that?"

"Okay. He's busy with work anyway. And I told him you need me."

Our waters arrive, and I squeeze a lemon wedge into mine.

"You don't have to stay, you know."

"I know, but I want to."

I stay quiet and look at her. How many times have we sat like this, across from each other, in various restaurants, talking and laughing or making observations?

During one of those lunches I talked to her about meeting Peter and how excited I was. She dragged every detail out of me, and I enjoyed re-telling the story of our first encounter because I re-lived it. My eyes were cloudy with my newfound love and anticipation of what the future held. I told her about his good-looking friend, Joseph, and how it would be wonderful if they met.

"Is he really cute? You know I don't like to waste my time," she said as she reached for her cocktail and took a sip, leaving red lipstick on the rim.

"Yes, he's cute," I responded. "Think: tall; messy, dark black hair; full lashes; almost pouty lips, like they're always ready to kiss you; and thick, broad shoulders."

"Oh wow! Sounds like you took more than a little look at him."

I laughed. "You're right; I did. But, only because I

was casing him out for you."

"Sure. Well, I don't want to wait. When can I meet him? Today?"

"Whoa! Hold your horses, missy."

"No ma'am. With that description, I want him now," she said slapping the table in mock urgency. We finished that meal happy with cocktails and laughter.

***

I can't say the same for this meal. I'm not like I was then. I'm bordering on desperation and depression, and I feel like the burden is mine to carry, so I won't share much with her.

I take dainty spoonfuls of my chicken Florentine, not because I'm trying to be proper but because I don't have much of an appetite.

"Liana, my dear friend, please tell me how I can help you."

I put down my spoon and look out the window. My reflection comes to me and shakes me. My hair hasn't been cut and styled since last summer. My eyes have become too small for their sockets; my cheekbones are more pronounced. At one time, I could have said I was pretty. I could have afforded a little vanity. I can't do that now.

I feel Daisy's hand on mine and I force my eyes from my reflection and onto her. In that moment, I want to hate her and her beauty, her freshness, and her naiveté.

"How can you possibly think you can help?" I ask flatly.

Her mouth falls open.

"How can you begin to think that you can understand? You've never had a worry in your life. Everything has always been easy for you. And if something doesn't work out just the way you want it to, you change it. I can't do that," I say. "Life is *not* a fairy tale for me. Life is hard work and hurt and soon . . . letting go." I choke on my words.

She closes her mouth and refuses to look away from me. Her hand is still on mine, her mouth is quivering faintly. She blinks several times and takes a slow, deep breath.

"Is that really what you think?"

I break eye contact.

"Life is not as easy for me as you think it is. I cry myself to sleep most nights because I'm so full of regrets. I used to look at you and wish I could have a happy steady life, like yours. And I thought I had that—with Joseph. But he wanted kids. He wanted forever. I wanted it too, so badly that it scared me, and I ran." She looks past me, as if she's seeing her past.

"Daisy, I . . ."

She holds up her hand, stopping me. "To this day I can't forgive myself for giving up the one man that I have truly loved. I drink to forget him, but all I can do is remember every single one of his kisses and the way he used to touch me. I've never been able to find that again, and I never will because there's no one like him. And now that I saw him again," she pauses, "you have no idea how badly I want him."

I reach for her hand with both of mine. "Daisy . . . I'm sorry. I didn't mean to upset you. I had no idea. Why didn't you ever say anything?"

"Because I didn't want you to think I was weak. And because I know that I can't change anything. I'm still *me*. Free-spirit and all," she says, waving her arm dismissively. "However much good that's done me."

We sit in silence, staring at soups that are getting cold.

"We sure are messed up, huh?"

"Sure are," she replies, and we smile.

I look at the time. "I gotta get back to work," I say; and together, arm in arm, we walk back to the library, where we hug and forgive each other for our little outbursts.

"Are you going to talk to him?" I ask. "Try to get back together?"

"No," she says quietly.

My heart relaxes, and I frown not understanding why it had constricted in the first place.

"I can't do that to him. He deserves to be happy. I can't give him that, even though I love him with all my heart."

"Why not?"

"I don't know. I guess because I'm me and he's him. It doesn't work. I'll never change."

I hug her tightly—strangely grateful for her honesty—give her a kiss on the cheek, and walk back in to work.

***

A few days later, Peter is in the bedroom listening to music and dozing off. I bring out my letters and spread them out on the kitchen table. One by one I pick them up and read them.

I'm deep in words, when a knock on the door brings me out of my reverie. I open the door to find Daisy holding a plastic grocery bag containing, from what I can see, a big tub of vanilla ice cream.

"Thought we needed to get lost tonight," she says and smiles.

"It might need to be stronger than that."

"I thought so," she says, and holds up a bottle of vodka which she'd been hiding behind her back.

I beam at her, taking the bottle. "Well, come on in!"

We walk to the kitchen table, which I failed to clean up.

"What's all this?" she asks, looking at my letters.

"Nothing," I say and hurriedly try to pick them up, but I'm not fast enough.

She picks one up and begins reading:

"Liana,
Today I must borrow words to speak to you, for my mind fails to produce anything worthy of you. Please forgive my clumsiness and take these words as a present. A present from my heart to yours."

"Please, stop," I whisper, and reach for the letter. I don't want to snatch it from her—I don't want to risk tearing it—but I don't want its secrecy to be ruined. It's mine and only mine.

She must sense my urgency because she hands it over, saying: "Fine, here you go." As she takes the ice cream and cans of cherry soda out of the bag, she adds, "Peter sure is sweet."

"They're not from him," I respond softly, as I turn from her and grab two mason jars. I bite my lip. I shouldn't have said anything. I should've let her assume.

She exclaims, "Liana! You? What's going on?" Her voice takes on a suspicious note.

I take my time to turn back around. She's staring at me wide-eyed and intrigued. I mentally kick myself.

"Liana? What's going on?"

"Nothing," I tell her, avoiding her eyes.

"Come on, Liana. It's me. You can talk to me. Are you seeing someone?"

"No!" I exclaim, handing her a couple of spoons and opening the bottle of vodka.

"Then, what's going on?"

She's not going to let me off-the-hook. "They're just letters I've been getting."

"From?"

Sighing, I confess, "I don't know."

"You must have some idea," she probes as she mixes a little of the cherry soda with vodka into the jars.

"I really don't have a clue."

She eyes me unconvinced.

I sigh. "Okay." As I pace, I tell her, "I'm not sure, but there's this one guy who goes to the library. He's a writer, and he loves poetry—very well spoken and handsome. He's always pleasant and looks at me like he's trying to tell me something special. At first, I was convinced it was him, but the last time I saw him, it was like—there was nothing there."

"Hmm . . . What do you mean, nothing?" she asks, adding heaping scoops of ice cream to the jars.

"I didn't feel anything. Not a rush. Not a flicker. Not a thing. If it's him, then I'm not attracted to him. I would be greatly disappointed."

"If it's not him, whoever it is, is head over heels for you. I didn't know people still did things like that. I thought romanticism was dead."

"Not for everyone," I say.

"Obviously. It is terribly romantic." She licks the back of the ice cream scoop and wistfully asks, "Why can't I find a guy who talks to me like that?"

"That's because you barely give them a chance to talk," I tease.

"You're right. I'd rather find out how they kiss," she purrs with a you-caught-me grin.

"You're incorrigible," I giggle.

"That's why I'm so much fun. Cheers."

I take my jar and lead the way to the living room. She brings the bottle with her, and we dig into our boozy cherry vanilla floats.

"Wow, this is delicious. Where'd you learn how to make these?" I ask.

"You remember Keith?"

"Which one, the first or second one?"

"That's right—there were two!" she laughs. "The one I went on the cruise with."

"Oh, yeah."

"He made these one day after we'd gotten back to our room and after we'd—you know. He said he had a new recipe he wanted to try. He walked out of the room in his Adam suit and then came back with one of these. And now I indulge every now and then . . . without the sideshow, though," she sighs dramatically.

"Ewwww. You didn't have to tell me all of that," I say dissolving in laughter. "Whatever happened to him?"

"Last I heard, he was married and on his way to fatherhood. Glad it wasn't me."

I take a long sip of my drink.

"How are things going with Danny?"

She added more vodka to her jar and put a tablespoon of ice cream in her mouth before answering.

"I haven't called him."

"Why not?"

She wouldn't look at me.

"Is it Joseph?" I don't want her to say that it is, even though I know the answer.

She sighs.

"Do you still have feelings for him?" I ask.

"I didn't think I did. I mean, how long have we been divorced? And I've been traveling all over the world, having loads of fun. Then I come back and see him, and it's like I never left. Like I need to be with him."

I open my mouth to talk, and she stops me.

"I know, I said it wouldn't work between us, but I can't help but wonder, what if?"

We both look at our now-empty jars.

"Want another?" she asks reaching for the bottle of vodka.

"Sure."

She goes to the kitchen and I turn on the radio while she's gone; trying to untangle my thoughts. Why do I get so protective when I talk to her about Joseph?

I turn up the volume, just enough to cover up my thoughts, and the room is filled with The Police:

"Every little thing she does is magic,
Everything she do just turns me on,
Even though my life before was tragic,
Now I know my love for her goes on . . ."

Daisy returns with two more floats. "I love that song," she exclaims, wiggling her hips. "Wasn't that in that movie; the one with Drew Barrymore?"

"Which one?" I ask, taking my jar from her and sitting.

She snaps her fingers when it comes to her. "The Wedding Singer."

"I don't think so."

"Yes it was. In that scene where Adam Sandler realizes he's in love with her."

I pretend to think on it. "Nope, don't recall."

"Well, then . . . we'll just have to watch the movie and find out. How about this weekend?" She suggests, taking a seat beside me.

"Maybe."

"Come on. I'll even throw in another concoction."

I smile in response—non-committed.

Drinking and thinking; we wait for the song to end.

PETER

I was born in the spring. The season of re-birth, of new beginnings. A time when the world finds its colors once again. But it's February now, and I'm sure that the spring I saw last year will be the last for me. I feel the end getting closer and, although I'm sad, I'm not scared anymore.

Sometimes when I'm sleeping I have dreams or visions. Today, I'm running behind a child on a bicycle. I'm holding on to the seat, like I'm training him. I can't tell if he's the boy I didn't have, the brother I lost, or the kid that I was.

Sometimes I see myself dancing with my mother—sometimes in the clouds, other times in our kitchen. Sometimes I'm laughing with Liana, other times I just get to watch her from afar. Sometimes she's mine, sometimes she's not.

The other day, I was the preacher who was marrying her off to someone else. Sometimes I really hate my dreams.

***

"Look what the cat drug out," my father says, walking into the bedroom for a visit. I can't believe who's walking in behind him.

"Bobby Joe," I say fondly.

He's changed, of course, from the last time I saw him. Back then, we had runny noses and skinned knees. Now he's tall, a little round in the waist; and he wears a full beard and glasses.

"Peter," he says and walks over to shake my hand.

My father points to the door, excusing himself. "I'll let you two catch up." I watch him walk away, then turn to Bobby Joe.

"Where have you been?" I ask smiling.

"I moved over to Virginia for a while. I came back a few days ago and my mom told me," he says, not looking away from me. "How are you holding up?"

"Just fine," I say, gesturing for him to sit.

"Are you taking chemo?" he asks, sitting across from me.

"No, it was too late for me."

"Oh."

"Don't worry."

"What kind?"

I've been so ashamed about what's killing me, I haven't really talked about it. Maybe it's time that I do. Instead of answering, I watch as the light coming in from outside dulls for a moment—a cloud must've passed before the sun—then it's bright again.

Bobby Joe scratches his chin, a clear sign that he's thinking.

I silently count to three, then I whisper, "Breast."

He sits up a little taller. "Excuse me?" he asks leaning towards me.

"Breast cancer," I repeat somewhat firmer.

I tell him how I discovered it, how it was diagnosed, how it was too advanced for treatment having traveled to other vital organs, poisoning me slowly until it is finished with me. How the only thing I can do is take incrementing doses of morphine to help manage my pain. He listens quietly, taking it all in.

My father walks back in. I try to lighten the mood.

"So, Bobby Joe, are you married?" I ask, attempting to sit up straighter.

"Yup, been married for about two weeks now," he gushes, handing me a pillow.

"Congratulations, man! Who's the lucky gal?"

"You remember Kenny?" he asks.

"Yeees," I reply, somewhat unsure of where this is going.

"Not him!" he chuckles. "His sister, Josie."

"His sister? The only sister I knew of was like in the third grade when we were graduating."

"That's the one."

"Oh. Where is she?"

"She's outside with Liana and Vivian," my father interjects.

"I'll go get her."

"No need to do that. I'll go out there," I tell him. And, slowly I shuffle out to the living room; my father behind me, ready to support me, if needed.

***

Bobby Joe and I regale everyone with stories of our shared childhood. He says something, I watch as Liana throws her head back laughing, her neck elongated and her eyes closed.

I become irritated with him. My head screams that that should be me, making her laugh. He tries to engage me again, but I'm done with him and with trying to converse. I sit there sulking and enjoying the confused looks my attitude is garnering.

He tells everyone he's an inspirational speaker, so now I'm somewhat intimidated by him. I think I want him to leave. Soon after that thought, I get my wish.

Liana walks everyone to the door, and extends an invitation to return whenever they wish. I grumble in discontent.

She closes the door and I mumble, "Glad they're gone."

Liana turns to me, puzzled. "What do you mean?" she asks as she begins to pick up cups and dishes. There's a big bowl with smeared remnants of banana pudding. Vivian had made it. She carries that to the kitchen and returns.

"Didn't you have a good time?"

"Apparently not as good a time as you," I spit out.

She stops looking for something to clean. "What is that supposed to mean?" she demands with her arms crossed across her chest.

"Nothing," I say, setting my jaw stubbornly.

"Nothing?" she asks, her voice dripping with barely controlled anger.

Stop this I order my thoughts, but I charge on. "I saw how you were hanging on to every word Bobby Joe said."

"He was talking to all of us!" she yells, throwing her hands up.

"But, I saw you *looking* at him. You couldn't even respect the fact that I was here, or his *wife*!"

Her head snaps back and tears slowly fill her eyes.

I demand sanity and control of my mind. I tell it

that I should stop this nonsense. That she really did nothing wrong.

"You like him. Don't you?" I accuse.

"Of course I liked him. He was *nice!*" she yells, still holding on to her tears.

And I want to reach out and make them disappear; tell her that I'm sorry, but in my agitated state I can't stop. Not yet. "That's not what I mean and you know it."

She squares her shoulders and calmly says, "You are unbelievable. After all I do for you day in and day out; after being here for you—this is what I get." Then, in an even softer voice she adds, "I didn't have to stay, you know."

This I know to be true and out of anger, defiance or plain stupidity, I yell scratchily, "Then go! I don't need your help! I'm fine without you!"

She grabs her keys and walks out the front door. All I do is watch her walk away, and then I apologize to the closed door and the empty room around me.

LIANA

Angrily I step on the accelerator and drive away from home. I furiously wipe away the tears that are falling hurriedly down my face. I turn down streets; some I know, some I don't, and before I know it, I stop the car. I fold over the steering wheel, and weep uncontrollably.

A knock on the window startles me. When I look up, I register Daisy trying to open the door and mouthing. I unlock the door, and she immediately reaches for me and pulls me into her arms. Without a word she begins walking, and I follow. Turns out I had parked in front of her house.

We sit on the couch, she hands me a box of Kleenex, and I tell her everything. When I'm done, I feel empty.

"I'm so sorry," she hiccups.

I look away and clench my fists. "I don't know why he's being such a jerk."

"I think you do know," she tells me calmly.

"But, why does he have to turn against *me*?" I argue back.

"Because you're the one he loves the most, and that's usually who we hurt the most."

Indignant I ask her through clenched teeth, "Are you siding with him?"

"No. I'm siding with what I know is really in your heart," she states gently and reaches for me.

I lean back frustrated—not allowing her to touch me—because I know she's right, and I don't want her to be right. I want her to rant and rave with me. I want her to confirm that Peter is a heartless bastard. I don't want her to be sensible and grounded. But, even through my angry outburst, I realize that *what* she is is just what I need.

"Why don't you stay here tonight?" she suggests. "We can call Joseph and have him stay at your house, in case Peter needs help."

I scan the immaculate room and briefly visualize a night away. The pull is magnetic. The lure of giving up is intoxicating. I can almost feel my body drifting into a wave of detachment.

"Does Joseph still have the same number?" Daisy cuts through my thoughts.

Untangling my body from the fantasy, I stand. "No, no. I can't do that. I've gotta go back."

"Liana . . ." she stresses, following me.

I stop by the door and turn to her saying, "The less people that know about this, the better.

***

I pull into my driveway with the headlights off. I can't believe I'm back, and I have to convince myself that what I'm doing is the right thing to do. I close my eyes and search for the man I fell in love with. The one with the sad eyes and slow smile. The one that made my heart leap with just the sight of him. But, all I can see is a thin outline of that man, a blur on the horizon; like when day is pushed out of the way by night.

I allow my heart to put my body into motion. It guides me through the door and into the cave of my love. Cold, hidden, lost. Covered in muck; distortioned by time. Destroyed by indifference.

I decide not to go to him. I'm here; that will have to be enough. I take off my shoes and lie down on the sofa. My heart weighs down in my chest. It doesn't pump just blood, it pushes deep-rooted tears out of my system. Choking on those tears, I wait for oblivion to take me.

The sun wakes me, and blinking against it I sit. I shower and change in the guest bathroom—I still don't want to see him. Although, I know that it's almost time for his medicine and he'll need something to eat with it.

Methodically, I make oatmeal and after several deep breaths, outside the bedroom door, I walk in. He's lying on his back and opens his eyes when he hears me.

"You came back," he whispers, trying to sit up.

I ignore the comment.

"Liana . . ."

I don't respond. Instead, I help him sit and hand him his breakfast tray.

"Will you sit with me?" he asks. "I want to talk to you."

I make myself look at him. "I've got things to do," I respond sadly, and walk out the room.

***

"Anybody home?" asks Joseph as he opens the front door.

I'm in the laundry room sorting clothes, listening to the radio which is playing from the kitchen. I was deeply lost in Dan Hill's "Sometimes When We Touch," that I didn't hear him knock. I try to wipe the melancholy from my face and clear all emotion from my voice.

"In here," I say stepping into his line of sight, still carrying a face towel.

"Oh, hey. The door was slightly open," he tells me. "Look what I brought." He holds out Billy Joel's record, *Glass Houses;* a huge grin on his face. We both know that Peter's favorite song is on there.

"You think he'll like it?"

I smile reaching for it. "He'll love it."

"I also grabbed your mail on the way in." He flips the record over and the mail is now on top, with another letter for me—winking at me through the stack of correspondence. Why do I keep forgetting to check the mail when I don't work? And why does he keep bringing it in? I grab the whole pile, and our fingers touch.

He grabs me by the arm. "Liana, you're shaking. What is it?"

"Nothing," I say, setting everything on the kitchen table; and in the next breath . . . "Everything."

"Come here," he says and puts his arms around me. Oh my! How good it feels to be held. I grab hold of his jacket, take in his smell, register his strength, and allow myself the moment of comfort. His embrace lifts some of the burden that has been weighing me down; that has had me marginally stagnant and almost obsessively depressive.

And, right now, I don't care if he saw the envelope or not. If he did, he wouldn't know what it is. Unless . . . No. It couldn't be him! He's our friend, mine and Peter's. He wouldn't do that . . . Would he? Does he see me as a woman or as his best friend's wife? Oh my goodness! I'm going crazy in my desperation.

He strokes my hair; I breathe him in, and lean into

him. I should step away but I can't.

The radio is still on and I hear Lynn Anderson singing:

"I beg your pardon, I never promised you a rose garden, along with the sunshine, there's gotta be a little rain sometime . . ."

And I think, I sure have had my share of rain; I want sunshine.

He reaches for my chin and makes me look at him. The music fades away. He is extremely strong and astoundingly handsome, something I've noticed before but hadn't dwelled on. His face comes closer to mine; I slide my arms up around his neck, and feel his muscles tense. I grab a fistful of his hair.

I can feel both our heartbeats racing, chasing, discovering. His eyes are searching deep within mine. I lean my face toward his and his lips brush mine. I feel like I'm going to melt. I swallow some of my hunger and kiss him. His lips are full and sweet, and I close my eyes and arch into him. He buries one of his hands in my hair; his other arm tightens around my waist as he deepens the kiss.

When our lips finally part, he rests his forehead on mine and I'm flooded with words from my letters. Could they be Joseph's? I read in my mind . . .

I am going out of my mind with the desire to be near you, to touch you.

Could that be him? I reach up to his lips again, not taking my eyes off of his. Our breathing is erratic, and this time our kiss is desperate, hungry, heated. I pull on his lip with my teeth. He groans and gives me back as much as I take. I push my hands under his shirt and feel his heated skin. He pulls me closer, tighter.

I fear I am deeply, irrefutably in love with you.

I pull back and see myself in his eyes. Is that love I see there? Then I turn away from him and cover my burning lips with my hand. What did I just do?

I feel him behind me.

Long into the night, I think of you.

"Liana," he says, softly touching my arm. I think I'm going to pull away—in fact, I know that I should—but I don't. I let his hand brand me. Am I really in love with him, or is it loneliness I feel? Is it because of how often I see him that my heart is confused? Is what I'm feeling, right now, real or a figment of my imagination?

He turns me around to face him. "Want to talk about it?" he asks, holding my quivering chin with his hand. His face is so honest and uncertain. He looks as lost as I am. This is not something he planned.

I hide my face in his chest and let my tears fall. He holds me tightly, and I realize he's crying too. He feels so sturdy and right and human, experiencing and understanding what I'm feeling. I hold him tighter.

"It's okay," he says, stroking my hair. "Will you forgive me?"

I laugh quietly and look up at him.

"What is there to forgive?"

He reaches for the hair that's fallen over my face and pulls it back behind my ear, blistering every inch of my skin that he touches. His thumb slides back until it reaches my lips. My heart stirs, and the realization of why I've been feeling so protective of him—around Daisy—hits me hard.

"I shouldn't have kissed you like that," he says.

"No, you shouldn't have," I whisper. "But you did."

"What now?" he asks, removing his hand from my face.

"What now?" I repeat.

I lay my head on his shoulder and let him hold me, hearing over and over and over in my mind, "What now?"

Peter coughs faintly from the bedroom.

"I'll go," he says.

As soon as he takes his arms from me, I feel lonely

and cold. Like he took the warmth with him as he walked out of the room.

I feel the need to occupy myself so I won't dissect every moment of those kisses. So I start on dinner. I take a nice, plump butternut squash and cut it into big chunks. I oil a baking sheet and set the squash on it; then I put it in the oven. *(My mind begins to work against me, and; I feel him beside me).* I peel carrots at the sink and cut them into thick circles. *(I feel him touch me).* I add them to a sauce pan with water, garlic and thyme. *(I feel his lips on me).*

As soon as the squash is tender, I take it out and put it in the blender. *(I hear him whispering my name).* Then I add the cooked carrots with a splash of the water I cooked them in, and pulse until a thick, creamy soup is produced. *(His lips are on my neck).* I put the soup into a saucepan and add a splash of milk. I rub my neck as I wait for it to boil, closing my eyes and seeing him. *(So much for not wanting to think).*

I smell the soup and hear it bubble and pop. Trading my moment of dreams with reality, I begrudgingly open my eyes. I scoop a miniature serving into a bowl for Peter, set it on a tray with a glass of water, and compartmentalize my feelings before I walk to the bedroom with his food. Hopefully he'll eat, and my guilt won't radiate off of me.

PETER

I'm not sleeping. I hear movement in the room. I want to open my eyes but I can't; they feel so heavy. I'd give anything in order to be moving and well. To be able to sit outside at night surrounded by the annoying sound of cicadas; or to be drenched in the midst of a cool spring rain; or to have my chest hurt from the carbonation of an ice-cold Coke.

There's more movement, and then Billy Joel's voice comes softly from the speakers. It's my favorite album.

I hear "It's Still Rock and Roll to me," and I feel my arms folding over my guitar; I get lost in the way I'm following the music. I'm rocking away on stage. The band is electrified, and I get my solo. I'm playing with Billy, and he's pointing at me like I'm killing it. I look out to the crowd; they worship me. I'm on top of the world. Me, my guitar, and Billy.

"Look, he's crying," I hear Liana say.

"He must be awake," replies Joseph.

I try to open my eyes again. But I'm tired.

"I brought him some soup."

Joseph comes close to me. "Peter," he says.

I grunt to let him know I hear him.

"Liana brought you your dinner; you want to sit up?"

I force my eyes open and nod once, slowly.

"Here, I'll help you," he says, putting one arm on my back and using the other to pull me into a sitting position. Liana puts pillows behind me to help me stay upright.

I glance to the record player. Billy's still singing to me. I look at Joseph.

"Thanks," I say hoarsely, and clear my throat.

He squeezes my arm.

Liana scoops a small spoonful of orange soup and goes to feed it to me. I open my mouth and swallow. Hand and foot service, I think, and get choked up. I start coughing; she's there quickly, with a rag to help cover my cough, and she rubs my back until the spell is gone. I lie back onto the pillows.

"Water?" she asks.

I nod and Liana hands me the glass. I can tell she's still upset by her shortness with me. When my mouth is moist again, I look at Joseph and ask, "So what have you been up to? When are you going to bring that girl around you mentioned? Juliet? Was that her name?"

I see him look at Liana and their glance averts quickly.

"I don't think that's going to work out," he says, fidgeting.

"Why not? Is it because of Daisy?"

"No . . . It's complicated," he tells me, removing the pillow that was stranded on the chair by the bed, and sits.

Liana tries to feed me more soup. I don't really want it but I take it. It's not long before I feel like I can't have any more. I turn away from the spoon. She removes the tray, setting it on the dresser.

The song changes. Liana removes the pillows she had used to prop me up with and, I close my heavy eyes. I hear them walking out the door and then closing it, and I whisper to the stifling silence how much I love her.

I concentrate on the music: "All for Leyna."

"There's nothing else I can do,
Cause I'm doing it all for Leyna
I don't want anyone new
Cause I'm living it all for Leyna
There's nothing in it for you
Cause I'm giving it all to Leyna . . ."

The music stops and I'm still awake. I enter the boxing

ring of my thoughts. And round and round I go. I'm throwing lazy punches and I'm getting suckered. Doubled over by the blow to my failed attempt at love.

The whole fiasco with my jealous outburst is still causing me to feel embarrassed. Liana doesn't deserve that kind of accusation, but even though I *know* that, I was still a jerk. She deserves a high-level of love. At first I thought myself capable of giving her that, and then I allowed my mind to talk me into my shortcomings. It convinced me that I wasn't enough, that she would find someone better in time. And instead of trying harder, I gave up. Not on her, on me. I thought I needed to protect my heart from impending doom. I was a jerk. And she's still here.

I feel like I've already said all of this before. I can't remember. There are lots of things that I'm beginning to forget. And I can't tell if other things are real or not. There are times when I open my eyes to find Liana looking at me quite strangely. As if I'd been talking in my sleep and the things I'd said weren't nice. It puzzles and scares me.

LIANA

feel Joseph following me. He sets the tray on the counter and rolls up his sleeves to rinse the dishes.

"Don't worry about it," I say. "Are you hungry?"

"Not really," he replies and sets his gaze on me. I want to look away but I don't. The kisses we shared are still fresh on my lips. Still simmering. I want him to hold me again, and in my mind I ask him to. He, in turn, puts his hands in his pockets. Hey, not all wishes are granted, and not all prayers are answered . . . right away.

"Would you like some hot chocolate?" I ask, opening the pantry.

His face breaks into a wide smile. "With marshmallows?"

"Sure," I say smiling back. "Why not?"

"That sounds perfect."

***

After he leaves, I pick up my letter and head to my chair. I can't open it, though. All I can think about is how Joseph kissed me. How he held me. How softly and deeply he touched me. Why did I allow this to happen? But, then again, how could I have stopped something I hadn't realized I wanted?

If I wanted to come up with an excuse, I could. I could say that Peter's sickness is wreaking havoc on all of our emotions. That we're both caught up in his care and decline. But I don't want to make an excuse. I don't want to cheapen what I felt . . . what I feel.

I open the envelope and unfold my letter, and this time while I read, it's Joseph's voice I hear, reading to me.

Liana,

I've started and stopped several letters. Some to tell you that it's the last time I'll write to you and others to tell you how crazy I am about you.

So I took a walk in the woods to try and calm my frenzied state of mind. I walked through the leaves, the breeze, and the silence. I walked through rows of oak trees and couldn't help but see you in them. Your strength, your resilience, your beauty.

You have been hammered by an incredible force, and yet you stand. You haven't looked for an easy way out. And your hand is gracious even when you're down.

As Lionel Richie sang, "You are once, twice, three times a lady," and your husband is a very lucky man.

Keep your chin up, you beautiful woman, you powerful lady; and don't lose your smile, because that is what makes my world go round.

With unyielding love,
Your admirer

I hiccup between my tears. How can this person see me like this? As *a beautiful woman, a powerful lady.* I certainly don't feel that way. What I do feel is my heart lifting and dipping. Soaring with this imaginary strength and scraping the bottom of the well of despair in quick succession. How can I feel so high and so low?

Why does love have to hurt so much? It's supposed to make a person happy. Irritated and confused, I bring my legs up to my chest and hug them crying into my knees. Darkness is my witness and my cover. It is the one that sets my sorrows free. If only it wouldn't give them back to me in the morning.

Why do my choices have to be so complex? It was so easy back when Peter and I met. My mind didn't have anything to do with my decision. My heart did the picking for me and I was elated. I went into the relationship with high hopes, with extraordinary dreams. I was going to be happy because my heart was happy.

When I told my mother about him—all gushing

and lightheaded with emotion—she quickly objected.

"But, mom, you haven't even met him. How can you say he's going to ruin my life?" I asked holding a pillow to my body to keep my hands from flying.

"Because he's beneath you," she responded without flinching.

"No, he's not."

"What does he do for a living?"

"He works on a farm."

"My point exactly. What kind of life is he going to give you? Look around you." She gestured to encompass my room. "You have everything you want. You need someone who will provide you with the things you're accustomed to."

I looked at the things my room held. The expensive furniture. The mounds of jewelry strewn above my dresser. My closet and drawers overflowing with clothes. Everything I thought I couldn't be without. But next to Peter, they were just things. They didn't matter.

"Life isn't about things, mom. It's about being in love," I countered throwing the pillow I'd been holding onto my bed.

"Oh honey. You're still so young," she said and tried to touch my cheek with her palm, but I moved away from her reach. Her hand dropped beside her. "Only the young and inexperienced think that love is all you need to make a life."

"You love Dad."

"Yes, but I was one of the lucky ones."

"Don't you want me to love my husband?" I challenged.

"Of course I do, honey. But that can come with time. You find someone with potential, and *then* you begin the journey to loving him."

"Well, that was how things were done in the past. Not now. Now, we have choices and the way I feel about him tells me that I can be very happy, even if it is in a small house and with inexpensive things."

"You have no idea what you're saying," she said; exasperation dressing her words.

"Yes I do. I'm not a child, Mother," I reminded her through gritted teeth. "I know the difference between love and infatuation. What I feel for Peter is definitely love and I'm going to be with him, no matter what."

"I really wish you would think things through. You would come to see that your father and I know better."

I groaned loudly. "Well, say what you will. I'm not a child anymore and you can't stop me."

"We'll see what your father has to say."

She hurried out of my room as if time was of the essence. I wanted to slam the door shut behind her, but I thought that would only prove me childish, so I closed it softly. Finally alone, I paced hastily; fuming—going over all the injustices I was facing, and I decided that neither time nor my parents would keep me away from the love of my life. My mother sent my father to put his foot down—not her best idea since he had too big of a soft spot for me—so in the end, I did what my heart told me to do. Peter and I married.

The first year was great. We couldn't get enough of each other. We had fun even if it wasn't wild, crazy love. Then during our second year of marriage his coolness became more evident; but I always had an excuse that would make it all okay.

If he didn't kiss me when he came home it was because he'd had a bad day at work. If he didn't tell me he loved me it was because he was distracted with chores. If he didn't make love to me regularly it was because he was tired. I always made justifications. He never had to make any because I never brought it up. I never asked him why.

I would tell myself that there were others who had it worse. They were abused, un-cared for. I had a beautiful roof over my head, and I never wanted for anything material. He'd come a long way financially. But my heart was making sacrifices and I was bending my soul around those sacrifices.

***

After I'm spent from my tears, I head to the shower. Slowly, I wash away the day and the film of sickness I'm wearing. I put on one of Peter's t-shirts and join him in bed. He's asleep, so I'm careful not to disturb him. I sit and watch him.

He's still beautiful. I feel the urge to trace his body with my fingers. I reach out and touch his hand which is cool to the touch. I move on to his chest which is rising and falling almost imperceptibly. I lay my hand over his heart and his steady heartbeat calms me.

I sit up on my knees and move on to his face. I use both of my hands to outline his features, touching him like a blind person would. I cover his face with both my hands. My fingers grace his eyebrows and cheekbones, and with my thumbs I outline his lips. They're a little dry, but still lovely. I lean into him and kiss his lips. Then I lie down beside him and put my arm around his waist.

Loving my husband, I fall asleep.

PETER

"I need to talk to Liana," I tell Joseph as we sit playing dominoes out on the patio.

"About?"

"About, after . . ."

Both of us are studying our tiles.

"Oh," he says setting down the double five tile, making me draw.

"I've tried to do so and she refuses to talk about it."

"Well, what have you said?"

I rub my chin and look up. "That she needs to promise me that she'll be fine and that she'll find someone to make her happy," I respond observing him, trying to determine if my suspicions are accurate.

He doesn't make eye contact. In fact, he's staring at his tiles so intently, that I reach a conclusion. I'm right. I feel it in my bones, and it doesn't break me.

I turn my face to the sky. It's mid-afternoon and

the sun is working to warm up the day, as winter fights back. The result is extremely pleasant. I'm looking for peace, and I find it—in the way the clouds move, the sun shines, and the earth endeavors to bloom again. The tail end of a playful breeze hits me and emotion fills me.

I focus back on Joseph and say, "It would make me very happy if that someone were you."

His jaw drops. "What?" he exclaims; almost knocking the chair over as he stands in a frenzy of shock.

I, on the other hand, am calm; as calm as a seal sunbathing by the ocean's edge. "I only say that because of how much I love both of you and if anyone could make her happy, I know it could be *you*."

He turns away from me. "You do realize," he says slowly shaking his head, "that isn't something you and I can plan."

"I know," I say. "But it sure would be nice."

The neighbor's kids are now playing outside, and it makes me wish—not for the first time—that I would've had children. Liana and I talked about it once, and decided it was better to wait. Now, the chance to hold a baby in my arms, to rock him to sleep and to be silly with, is gone.

"Have you told her that?" he says turning back to face me, blowing through the puff of longing I was in.

"No."

"Good."

"But, I did think about it."

"Well, don't," he tells me quietly.

"Why not?"

"Because . . ." He falters. "Because she's your wife."

I smile sadly. "Not for long."

"Don't talk like that."

"I wish I didn't have to, but I'm facing my *truth*, Joseph," I remind him stiffly.

He sighs.

Softening my voice I continue, "It was just a thought."

I lie back, and as he helps cover me I add, "She is beautiful and caring and loving and tender and a wonderful cook." I exhale slowly. "She's perfect."

"Shut up," he says, and hits me softly on my uncovered arm. "Go to sleep."

"I'm half-way there, my friend." I yawn and repeat, "Half-way there."

He leaves.

Church bells are ringing. A pitying of turtledoves cuts through the sky. The sun is shining brightly, its rays ricocheting off the earth. I hear laughter all around me. I stand in the middle of a field of wildflowers while my lungs fill to capacity with their perfume. Rocky Mountain columbines, sego lilies, buttercups, and dandelions all around me, forming what appears

*to be a comfortable pillow. I open my arms and allow myself
to fall back until I'm swallowed up by earth.*

Laughter and whispers wake me. There's been a steady stream of people coming and going. Sometimes I sit with them, sometimes I talk with them, and other times I sleep while they visit around me. I still move around but every step I take is labored. My breathing can become uneven or erratic. My appetite is diminishing. Most of my meals consist of some kind of mushy soup, pudding, or nutritional shakes.

Several conversations are happening, and I don't attempt to follow any single one. I feel like I've been transported to a circus stage. I'm on display. Everyone is here to see me. I'm the show. And I've been given the vanishing act.

I open my eyes. I see my mom.

"Momma," I whisper.

"Peter." She is unearthly beautiful, wearing a long, white dress. Her hair is parted down the middle, and her long, soft curls come around her shoulders, all the way to her waist.

"I'm so glad you came," I declare awestruck.

"Me too, sweetie," she says, walking toward me.

She takes my hand in both of hers. Then she touches my cheek; I lean into her soft palm. "How have you been, my sweet boy?" she asks.

"Not so good," I respond.

"Oh, baby," she says and takes my head and lays it on her chest. I relish the feel of her. I feel a breeze around us and her hair glides all around her. "It's okay," she whispers. "Momma's here."

"Yes," I say. "Momma's here."

She then kneels before me, like she used to when she would take the hair out of my face and kiss my forehead. She does that now. Her lips so gentle, so smooth. I lean into her. "What happened to your hair, baby?" she asks.

"It's gone. The cancer took it, and it's taking me, too."

She holds me tighter and kisses my head. Then she looks me in the eyes and says, "You're still as handsome as ever, you know."

I smile, because coming from her, I believe it.

She sits down beside me. "Who are all these people? Aside from your father. I know him," she says with a smile.

I look around. "Well, there's Joseph, my best friend; and his ex-wife, Daisy. And that's Bobby Joe, you remember him from across the way?"

She nods.

"That's his wife Josie," I continue. "And then there's Vivian, Eden, and Brae: Dad's new family." I pause waiting for a reaction from her, but she just smiles.

"He has a beautiful family," she concedes.

"And that lovely woman right over there, that's my wife, Liana."

I observe her as she talks with Daisy, Josie, and Vivian. I've never hit her, and yet I can see bruises all over her body, as if I'd inflicted fresh wounds, as if I had cut open her flesh and it's bleeding. All with my indifference. She looks defeated, nostalgic and un-happy. In a rare moment of altruism, I tell myself I need to set her free.

"Oh, Peter. She's beautiful. Just what I had envisioned for you. You did well, my son. You did well."

She lays her head on mine and puts her arms around me. I close my eyes and let her hold me.

***

I can't breathe. I feel my chest tightening. It's dark all around me. I put my hand out, I can't see a thing. I touch something. What is it? Where am I? Where is the light? I try to stand but I can't move. I hear crying. Who is that? Why are they crying? I hear a chain turning. I feel movement. I can't move but I feel myself moving. Descending. Then I hear a thud and more crying. What's happening?

Then it hits me. I'm being buried! I become frantic. I yell, "I'm alive! I'm alive!" No one hears. No one hears. I'm in a full panic. I thrash around. I need to knock on this box, loudly. I have to stop them. I must breathe!

***

"Peter, Peter. Wake up!" I hear.

And I think: Thank God! Someone heard me. Tears of joy spring to my eyes.

"Peter, sweetheart."

"Who is it?"

"It's me. I need you to calm down baby. Breathe."

"Mom?"

"Shhh." A hand rubs mine and that voice says over and over, "It's okay, baby, it's okay. It's going to be okay. Calm down."

Then I hear:

There shall no one come to harm thee
Naught shall ever break thy rest
Sleep my darling babe in quiet
Sleep on mother's gentle breast.

Sleep serenely, baby, slumber
Lovely baby, gently sleep;
Tell me wherefore art thou smiling
Smiling sweetly in thy sleep?

Do the angels smile in heaven
When thy happy smile they see?

Dost thou on them smile while slumb'ring
On my bosom peacefully.

It's the lullaby my mother used to sing to me. I've never
known the name of it. How in the world did I forget that?
I feel my breathing regulating to the sound of her voice.

"Go to sleep, baby. Everything will be okay."

LIANA

I hate being a care-taker, a care-giver, a whatever-it's-called. I realize how terribly awful that sounds, but it's the truth. It is devastating to watch the decline in him. Not just physically, either. I can't continue to take the times when he's hurtful. I try and try and it seems like I can't do anything right. The food is wrong, the room temperature's uncomfortable. It's even my fault that the water is tasteless!

I shouldn't talk like this. It's not that I mind helping my husband. Truth is, that's the only reason I still do this. I don't understand how some people have a *calling* to do this. I can only keep trying because I love him. Yes, even through my frustrations, I love him. It's the situation I get frustrated with, not him. After all, he is the one who has it the hardest, going from strong and self-sufficient to frail and dependent.

***

The day has come. The doctor has recommended hospice care. Peter says he wants to stay at home. He doesn't realize the moments of delirium he's having and that we're not properly equipped for his care, but he wants to be where his surroundings are comfortable. And I need to make sure he's comfortable.

It's now the end of February, and winter is waving a lazy goodbye, giving spring occasional moments of access to the world. In those rare instances, the sun is high and strong, and the wind is lethargic and cool, but it feels new. Like a turning tide, like a yapping puppy, like a stolen smile.

Today I've been waiting, nervous and defiant. A nurse or aide is coming over to tell us what to expect. I imagine pep talks and empty words coiling in my head, and I hate her already.

A car pulls up by the curb and I draw the curtain back, just slightly, so I can take an inconspicuous look. I see a blue car with white letters on the door that announce "Gentle Hands Hospice Care." Why do they have to broadcast to the world what they're doing at my house?

Joseph comes up behind me and lays a hand on my shoulder. He's my rock. We haven't kissed since that first time, and we're back to being just friends, caregivers.

He's here to help me cope and understand; at the same time that he's doing this for his own sake.

I watch as a woman comes up the sidewalk, then the stairs, and then she's in front of my door. I wait for her to knock.

"Hello," I say as I crack the door. I don't want to let her in because I feel like, as soon as she crosses the threshold, death will be dragged in on her heels.

"Hello," she says. "My name is Caressa from Gentle Hands Hospice Care." Her voice is tender, soothing.

She looks to be in her mid-fifties, is relatively plump; and her hair is short and dyed brown. I can see the gray roots. She hands me a card and when her hand touches mine, it's soft, like an overly washed blanket. I look at the card. Beside her name is the word "Owner." Her hands fit the name of her business.

"Are you Liana?"

I nod.

Joseph comes around me with extended hand, and they shake.

"I'm Joseph. Family friend. Please come in."

"Thanks."

She takes a seat on the nearest sofa and sets her briefcase down beside her.

I made coffee earlier, and its smell still swirls around in the air. I thought about baking cookies but then I stopped myself. This isn't a social call, I thought. I'm not meeting a friend. This is a person who is going to help me transition my husband from the living to the . . . gone.

"Would you like some coffee?" offers Joseph.

I'm grateful that he's taking the initiative to be hospitable, since I'm still quite numb from the realization that this is it. There's no other way to go. Everything that could have been done has been done. There's no detour. There's no chance of a different outcome. She's here now, it's going to happen. It's not a matter of if. It is now a matter of when.

"No thanks, but water would be great."

He leaves us alone, and I don't look at her until he returns.

"I understand that this is a very difficult time for you both. Not more than two years ago, I sat where you are, and thankfully someone came to help me find a way to cope and manage. That's why I am here today."

She takes out a pamphlet from her briefcase. It looks shiny and blue to match her car. She hands it to me. I don't open it. She doesn't seem to mind.

"One of the things I'll be doing is helping Peter with pain management. Is he still responsive?"

"Yes, he doesn't say much but he gets his point across," Joseph answers for me.

"Good. That will help. I will also ensure that you have all of the supplies and equipment needed for his care. I'll give you ideas on how you can help alleviate his pain while I'm not here. And . . ." She fixes her gaze on me. "I'm also here to give you some time off."

I look at her, appalled.

"It's okay," she says. "As caregivers, we need some time for us. You need some time for you. You need to walk outside and enjoy the fresh air. You need to be able to go to the hair salon, or to the store, or just rest. It's not selfish to do those things. On the contrary, it will help you care for him that much better."

I don't believe her.

"Are there any concerns you have?" she asks kindly.

Joseph looks at me as if asking for permission. I look away.

He says, "Lately, Peter's been talking to his mother a lot. She passed away when he was ten."

She's quiet for a beat before responding. "I see. Hallucinations are actually quite normal, and it's important to remember that for him his mother is quite real. The best thing you can do is talk calmly to him and give him reassurances."

She keeps talking. I know this because I see her lips moving, but I have now tuned her out. I watch her lips without a desire to read them. Her lips stop, and I feel Joseph's voice vibrating beside me. I don't hear what he's saying. It's like I'm watching a silent movie. But, where's the upbeat background music and the word cards? Those would be nice.

***

On our wedding day, after leaving the courthouse, we went to Santi's Bar and Grill. Joseph and Daisy were our only witnesses. I was wearing my wedding dress; a nice, simple dress made of soft, white cotton with a high, strapless, square neckline that reached my collarbone; a cinched waistline; and a calf-length flared skirt. My heels were four inches high with a strap across the toes and another one around my ankles.

I wore imitation pearls and felt like I had a million dollars strapped around my neck and wrist. My ears showcased their small companions.

I zoned into the music, Lobo's "I'd Love You to Want Me," as we waited for our food.

"When I saw you standing there
I 'bout fell out my chair
And when you moved your mouth to speak
I felt the blood go to my feet . . ."

Peter looked at me and I felt my heartbeat accelerate. He was now my husband. I rolled the word over in my mind, enjoying the sound of it. His ring sat on my left hand.

". . . Baby, I'd love you to want me
The way that I want you
The way that it should be"

My insides went all soft. I reached for his hand and couldn't wait to be alone with him. As we ate, drank, and talked, I couldn't stop glancing at Peter as we carried on a friendly conversation.

The more I looked at him and took in our new status, the more excited I got. My chest began heaving in nervous anticipation. I was hungry for him. My hands impatient to be on him.

I wanted to leave, but I sat there and waited. I had my whole life ahead of me to enjoy him. It would be me and him against the world, with nothing but love and time.

It might not have been the reception that most brides dream of, but it was perfect for me. The music was pleasing, the food was exquisite, and the company was meaningful. What more could I have possibly asked for? What more could I have possibly wanted?

The song changed; and to the sound of The Spinners' "Working My Way Back to You," I come out of my memory.

***

I'm groggy, like I just awoke from a deep sleep. I search the room, but I don't see Caressa.

"Where is she?" I ask.

"She went to check on Peter."

He reaches for my hand and asks, "Do you want to talk about where you went just now?"

"Our wedding day," I say, and my voice catches. I take a deep breath and exhale slowly. "I had such high hopes, thinking we were always going to be happy, always in love. I never thought that it could be any other way."

"What do you mean?" His forehead wrinkles in confusion. "He didn't make you happy?"

I let my head fall. "Yes, he did," I say. Then I think to myself, why am I lying? So I retract, "No, not for a while."

He raises my head and scoots closer to me. "What are you talking about?"

"Oh, it might sound trivial now."

"I'm sure it won't," he says, giving me confidence.

"It's just that . . . he was . . ." I search my brain for a good descriptive word. All I can come up with is, ". . . cold."

He kneads my knuckles. I watch his hands and I begin to relax.

"Before we married, he was always a little quiet and not very affectionate. I thought it was because he was shy and that he'd change once we were married and had time alone. Then I would notice that he would get this look in his eyes, like he wasn't even here with me. And he wouldn't touch me. I think and think, and I can't recall a single time when he said I love you to me, without me saying it first. A while back, I stopped saying it. He never asked why."

"But he's crazy about you," Joseph exclaims confidently. "He's told me so himself."

"Well, he hasn't told me," I say and catch myself when I hear how bitter I sound. "I hoped it was just a phase he was going through, with the melancholia and quiet spells. . . but I couldn't pull him out of it."

"I'm sorry Liana." He pulls me into his arms. "This takes me by surprise. The way he talked about you guys, it sounded like you had it made. Like no one could be as happy as the two of you."

"Really?" I ask, with a hint of sarcasm; pulling away from him.

He nods. "Did you ever tell him how you feel?"

I shake my head. "I guess I wanted him to pick up on my sadness and ask me about it. You know, to show that he was involved. That he cared about us."

It was his turn to shake his head. "Liana, men don't think that way. Most of the time, we need you women to tell us what it is we're doing wrong. He thought everything was fine."

Now I feel myself getting upset. I stand up and pace.

"Unbelievable," I say. "So I was supposed to say, 'Look Peter you're hurting my feelings and this is what you need to do to make things right'? Was I supposed to say, 'Will you bring me flowers today when you come home from work? Will you tell me I look beautiful and that no one else is as beautiful as me'?" I ball my fists, and question angrily, "Is that what I was supposed to do?"

He stands in front of me and puts his hands on my arms, calmly, making me stop. Then he pulls my hair behind my ear and, looking into my eyes he says, "That's not what I'm saying at all. I'll admit that we men can be ignorant when it comes to loving a woman. I also agree that every woman should have a man that tells her how beautiful she is. A man who's willing to put his heart in his hand for her every single day. A man who's willing to make a fool of himself in his eagerness to show his love."

"That's all I ever wanted," I concede, deflating. "I wanted to feel him love me. Not just physically, but deep down in my soul." Tears chase each other from my eyes.

"But he does, Liana," he tells me gently, wiping at the tears that are flowing hastily down my face.

"Then why hasn't he said so?" I sob.

He takes a step towards me—holds my face in his hands. A knock at the door shakes me. As I reluctantly take a step away from him, I wipe my face.

"Liana . . ." he whispers.

My heart hesitates; it forgets to pump and I go dizzy with emotion. He steadies me; his gentle touch moving from my arm—the point of contact—to my heart, jump-starting it. I lean into him, close my eyes, and breathe deeply. Then I make myself walk away.

"Are you ready?" Daisy asks as I open the door to her.

"Ready? For what?" I sniffle, still feeling slightly shaky from my tears.

Caressa comes into the room just then. She tells me the examination went well and that she'll be back tomorrow.

"I'm here to take you out," Daisy says as Caressa leaves. "What's wrong?" she asks, noticing my tear-struck eyes. She looks to Joseph and then back at me. "What's going on?"

My heart is in my throat, thumping in my ears. Joseph purposefully doesn't respond. I purposefully don't look at him.

"Nothing," I respond.

"Joseph?" she insists.

"Nothing, Daisy," he mutters. "Just drop it."

"Fine," she snaps at him. "Come on, Liana. Let's go."

"I can't go out," I protest.

She gives me a hard once-over. "Okay, I'll let you rest today, but I will be here for you tomorrow. No excuses!"

She turns on her heal and rushes out the door.

***

True to her word, she shows up the next day, and Joseph makes it a point to be in the bedroom, with Peter, when she arrives.

"Where are we going?" I ask.

"Somewhere fun."

I shrug.

Our first stop is the salon, where her hairstylist—Melina—cuts, colors, and styles my hair. Then I'm treated to a much needed pedicure. She also does my makeup for me.

The woman is loud and hilarious, and I laugh until my sides hurt. When we leave, my spirits have been greatly lifted. I feel pretty again. It's been a long, long while.

We stop in front of a nice dress shop called Elegance by Vani.

"What are we doing here?" I ask.

"I saw an outfit here the other day that will look wonderful on you."

"But I don't need new clothes," I protest half-heartedly.

"I know, but it'll be fun. Come on," she says and puts her arm through mine.

We walk in and she leads me to a display case on the far right side of the store. There's a stylish wrap-around dress on a mannequin. It's Peach silk with a brown straw belt, long sleeves, and a semi-plunging v-neck. Sitting under it are a pair of strappy, brown platform shoes.

"What do you think?" she asks me, smiling.

"It's beautiful," I say.

She finds one on the rack, that appears to be two sizes smaller than what I would have looked for, and she shuttles me to the dressing room.

"Come out when you have it on," she instructs, and leaves to do some browsing of her own.

Inside the fitting room stall, I slowly shed my overly worn clothes. I put the dress on and delight in the feel of the silk against my skin. I look at my reflection from all different angles and get caught up in how different I look. My hair is shorter, barely grazing my shoulders, and highlighted. My makeup is subtle, except for my eyes, which are outlined in black and shadowed in different shades of brown. The drabness of the recent months has been erased. I smile.

"You still in there?" I hear Daisy ask.

"Mmm, huh," I respond, still staring at myself.

"Here, put these on and let me see you."

She passes a pair of the brown platform shoes over the stall's door.

I feel like summertime. I can't stop smiling and I think that it's a good thing the day is warm. I step out of the dressing room feeling like a new woman.

She whistles. "Wow! Look at you! You look amazing. Turn around."

I give a full circle, letting the dress's skirt flow around me.

"That color looks great on you, honey," adds the dressing room attendant.

"What do you think?" asks Daisy.

"I think it's beautiful, but a little too much. I have nowhere to wear this."

"Nonsense, you're wearing that today, just for the heck of it."

"Would you like me to take the tags to the register?" asks the attendant.

"That would be perfect," says Daisy as I catch another glimpse of myself in the mirror.

At the register there's a long layered necklace with thumb-sized gold leaves along its sides; earrings and bracelet to match.

"Here, put these on," Daisy says. I take it she had already picked them out.

"But . . ."

"Uh-uh. Not going to listen." She even covers her ears playfully.

So I put them on, secretly luxuriating in how wonderful I feel.

The cashier hands me a bag holding my t-shirt and jeans, and then we walk back out onto the street. I am beautiful and confident. I pretend not to notice, but I see the men we pass staring; and I smile a big, I-can't-help-myself kind of smile. This is what Julia Roberts must have felt like in *Pretty Woman* after the shopping scene.

We walk into Ricky's Lounge and are directed to a small table, where we sit on couches and order mojitos.

"So what's this all about?" I ask.

"It's about you. You've given your heart and soul caring for Peter—so much so that you've put yourself in the backseat. So, I decided it was time for a little pampering and I have to say . . . you look . . . WOW!"

I laugh elated.

"Thanks," I say sobering up. "I did need this."

"I know," she says, and reaches for my hand. "Guess what?"

"What?" I ask taking a long, lazy sip from my mojito.

"I'm engaged."

I about choke. I cough. "You're what? To who? When?"

She laughs. "Yup, about the reaction I expected."

"Sorry," I say.

"It's okay. I would have worried if you hadn't been surprised."

"So, who is it?"

The waiter arrives and takes our orders. She finishes her drink and requests two more.

As soon as he walks away, she answers, "Danny."

"Really?"

"Yeah. We talked. He told me how he can't live without me; he just sounded so desperate . . . I had to say yes."

"No! Daisy, you wouldn't!"

She laughs. "No. This time apart has helped me see what he means to me."

"What about your feelings for Joseph?" I ask tentatively. My heart alert, beating furiously; as I try to project serenity, casualness.

"I don't think I'll ever get over him, but I'll be all right. He will find someone great to love, someone stable, and he'll finally have what he deserves. And I'm okay with that."

"Wow! I can't believe it. You're getting married." I know all my happiness is not because of her upcoming marriage, but I don't want to think what I'm thinking; and yet I do. "When?" I ask, to distract my thoughts.

"I'm flying back to Oregon this weekend, we'll work out the details and then I'll be back. He has such a huge family I'm not exactly sure how it's all going to work. But, enough about me. How about you? Any more letters?"

I shake my head.

"Oooh . . . The mystery," she teases. "Any ideas yet on who it is?"

Yes! I holler in my mind. "No, not a single clue."

"Mmmm. How romantic."

"I know, right?" I admit, and we giggle like silly schoolgirls.

I look toward the bar; I register a guy trying to get my attention, but all I can think about is the whirlwind of emotions I'm being hit with. Butterflies in my stomach, a tightening of my heart, and a head full of hopes.

***

When she drops me off at home, I'm a little giddy and tipsy. It's easy to do, when you haven't had a drink in forever.

I walk through the front door and Joseph is standing in the living room, as if he was walking back in from the kitchen.

He sees me and stops cold. "Whoa!" he says juggling a plastic cup in his hands and failing, dropping it to the ground, spilling its contents.

I blush.

"You look great," he says, regaining his composure.

"Thanks," I whisper, and reach for my now shorter hair, out of nervousness.

"I'll clean that," he says running to the kitchen.

I grab one of the towels I keep on the couch, and kneel to wipe up the spilt water.

He joins me a few seconds later; I've finished cleaning. He reaches for my hand to help me up. I accept his help, and as I stand I realize how close I am to him.

I reach out and touch his hair.

He pulls me closer.

"This color looks beautiful on you," he whispers in my ear, causing my arms to erupt in goose bumps and my legs to weaken.

He tightens his grip on me.

Peter coughs.

"Peter's awake," he says hoarsely.

I nod; my giddiness leaves me. Duty replaces it.

Joseph doesn't release me immediately. I look up into his eyes and then I break away from him, wishing Peter would've touched me and looked at me like that.

Maybe if he had, I wouldn't have felt so alone— with him.

PETER

Rain slaps against my window in a frenzy. The world appears to be in a rage. Thunder shakes the skies violently and lightning illuminates the murky night.

Liana is lying beside me, close but not enough to touch me. I reach in the dark, looking for her hand. When I find it, it's slack with sleep. I think about how her hands have fed me, cared for me . . . and how they used to touch me.

I never lost my desire for her, and I will die with that desire intact. No one else awoke that in me, before or after her. Even in her house shoes and pajamas, she is beautiful to me. And tonight, when I saw her walk in with that peach dress hugging her waist and barely touching her thighs, I felt my fingers tingling. She looked so beautiful, so sexy—I wished that I could get up off this bed and touch her. I would love to be able to run my fingers through her hair and kiss her neck, especially that one spot right underneath her ear that makes her sigh.

But my body is done with life, and all I can do is listen to the rain.

How many storms, like this have we gone through? One in particular comes to mind. It started quite early in the evening, and it wouldn't let up. Our electricity went out as we lay in bed. It was before I completely disappointed her. Before I broke her heart. Our love was still young, and I had touched her then, slowly, with purpose, until we forgot about the raging storm. Why did I ever stop doing that?

Did I begin my love journey thinking that I would turn cold? No. I thought that given a chance, I would always be happy. But once I had the opportunity in my hands, I folded into my insecurities and wrapped myself in a past that I refused to let go of. I allowed it to define me and I never tried to rise above it. I believed I wasn't worthy. In fact, I was sure that I wasn't. Even today, I can't say that I am.

Liana sighs beside me, and I wish I could touch her. But I can barely move. I am saddened to my bones, and I want to cry with the rain. She turns over in her sleep; and her hand lands on my thigh. I reach for it and bring it to my belly. Her face is now close to mine. I reach over and kiss her hair.

"I love you," I whisper. She's sound asleep. She doesn't hear.

I watch her face, illuminated with every lightning bolt, until the storm lets up; and then I go back to sleep.

***

I wake up with an ominous feeling. I know what it is. I can sense it. I look to Liana's side of the bed; it's empty. I hear her in the kitchen. Rolling over to her side of the bed, I take in her smell. I need all of her that I can get to face what lies ahead. Then I lie back and close my eyes.

"Get down from there before your father skins your hide!" my mother tells me. She's laughing when she says it, though, knowing full well that she won't let him see me.

She's pulling weeds from the garden. I'm supposed to be helping her. Instead, she gave me a ripe, candy-sweet peach; and now I'm sitting on a branch off our Utah juniper tree with my feet dangling beneath me, enjoying the juicy, messy peach.

I'm standing in the front line of our second grade class on stage. My mother is in the crowd, smiling and waving at me. I'm dressed up as a cowboy for our musical presentation. My class gets to sing, "Deep in the Heart of Texas." She seems proud and I stand up tall.

I'm running in long shorts and a well-worn t-shirt. Bob-

by Joe is running beside me and the neighborhood puppy, who we call Slappy, is on my heels. His tail is wagging and his long ears are flapping. I'm carrying a stick. Slappy barks; I stop, throw the stick, and watch him run after it.

I'm in my small apartment above the barn, learning how to play guitar. It's summertime, and though nights are normally short, for me they drag on and on. I try to tell myself I'm not lonely, but sadness takes ahold of me. I feel my heart clenching, asking for release. I convince myself that I will get out. That I will try to find the one my heart desires.

I've finally worked up my courage tonight, and I kiss her. I'm quivering inside. I still can't believe I'm holding her. If I wasn't feeling her breath against my skin, I would probably think I was dreaming. But she's here. She's the one for me. I'm absolutely sure of it.

I stand before her and a judge. I don't know what all he says; I'm lost in her eyes. We say yes, exchange rings, and I'm a married man. I'm elated. Nothing can beat the way I feel right now.

I broke her heart tonight. I can see it in her eyes but she doesn't say anything to me. I don't apologize. I can't even remember why I was so upset. I see the tears escaping her eyes. I walk away and try to pretend that I didn't hurt her.

The last bits of my hair are coming down. I asked Joseph to shave my head because my hair is now so thin. I'm plastered to my bed, a permanent fixture on this mattress, an outline on the bedsheets.

My father and I are standing face-to-face, neither of us speaking. His family stands a few steps behind him.

Joseph and I are walking down Main Street. Now we're playing music. Now we're fishing. Now he's sitting beside me as I waste away. Always there. Always with me.

This has been my life. A lifetime of memories, in a span of a few seconds. This is me.

"Are you ready baby?" I hear my mother ask me.

I sigh coming out of my memories. No. I can't go. Not just yet. There's something I must do first. I open my eyes and look to my right. Liana's writing desk is there, a few steps from me. I pray and find a burst of strength rush through me. I sit up slowly; then I stand. And on wobbly colt legs, holding on to my dresser, I make it to her desk.

I sit, catch my breath and begin to write.

My dearest Liana,

This is the last letter I am able to write to you.
Forgive me baby. Find love. Be happy.

I love you,
Peter

Tired from this effort I close my eyes and lay my head on the desk, on top of my letter.

LIANA

"That storm last night sure was a bad one," comments Joseph, emerging from the guest room.

When Daisy dropped me off last night, it was already starting to rain. By the time Joseph was preparing to leave, it was a full-blown storm. I suggested he take the guest room, and he had readily accepted.

"Half the town is without electricity," he informs me.

"I didn't even hear it," I say as I fill the coffee-pot with water.

"That must have been some sleep you were in."

"It sure was. It's been a while since I slept so soundly."

"You look nice," he says abruptly. "I like what you did with your hair."

I blush and reach for my hair. "Daisy made me cut and style it. I didn't think it was necessary, but she talked about how raggedy I was looking," I say and laugh.

"I bet Peter couldn't stop looking at you."

"He did tell me I looked nice," I say and smile sadly at the floor. I shake my head and decide I'm not going to be sad today. "Would you like toast or pancakes?" I ask.

"Pancakes. Do you have blueberries?"

"No, but I have bananas."

"Bananas? For what?"

"Banana walnut pancakes," I answer reaching for the flour in my pantry. "You've never had any?"

"Nope, can't say that I have. But I have a feeling I will, huh?"

"Yup. I'll even let you help me make them."

"Yay," he says with mock sarcasm.

Laughing, I ask, "Do you mind if I turn on the radio? I find it easier to work while I listen to music."

"That is quite all right with me."

I flip on the switch and am glad to hear an upbeat song playing. Elvis Presley is telling the world how he "Got Lucky." I feel like dancing as I cut a banana into bite-size pieces and fold it into my pancake batter. I add finely chopped walnuts, a dash of cinnamon, and then I start making buttery, golden pancakes. Joseph cooks sausages and coffee brews in its pot.

The radio DJ must be feeling good today too. Now the Bellamy Brothers are on with "Let Your Love Flow." I want to turn the volume up high and dance until I fall over from exhaustion. Instead I look out the window. Leaves are strewn about and my flower bed looks like it was trampled on. Puddles of water have collected in the yard. The sun is shining bright, not a tiny indication in the skies of the storm that passed us by.

"Look," I say, pointing. "There's a rainbow. I haven't seen one of those in forever."

Joseph stands beside me, and we watch the colors that are cutting through the sky, arching into the earth, bringing with it the promise of a better day. We sit down to eat. I look at Joseph, and smile. Yeah, today I feel good.

The radio moves on to Fire Fall, "You Are the Woman."

"The DJ must be in love," I remark.

"I was thinking that too," he replies.

"There's nothing like the oldies, huh?" I say.

"That's exactly what Peter would say."

"Sure is."

I butter up my pancakes and cover them in warm maple syrup. I watch as Joseph does the same. He takes his first bite as I'm cutting my sausage.

"Wow! I'm impressed," he says. "I wasn't sure I was going to like these, but they are delightfully great."

"Thanks. I kind of just made them up."

"No way," he says as he takes another bite. Once he swallows he asks, "Do you make recipes up often?"

"Sometimes," I answer shyly.

"You should do so more often. Maybe even write a recipe book."

"Thanks," I say. "But I'm not *that* good. I'll leave that to the professionals."

We finish breakfast and I pour myself a second cup of coffee, add my sugar and milk, and offer him the pot. Then I mash up a half of a banana for Peter, and grab a glass of water.

Before I walk out of the kitchen, I watch as Joseph breaks out a set of sorry moves to Wild Cherry's, "Play That Funky Music" while he works to clear the table. I laugh out loud and think that it's nice to feel happy. The shadow of death has left us. Softly I walk back to the bedroom, where I left Peter sleeping. I hate to wake him, but it is time for his medicine.

When I woke up this morning, I had my arm across his waist and he had his hand on my arm. It was nice to feel him like that. I also had the vague sensation that he had told me he loved me. I wasn't sure if I dreamed it, but it sure felt good.

I open the door smiling, ready for a better day than those we've had. Today I will talk to him. Today I will tell him that I love him, that I always have and I always will. Today I will let him know that our life together has been a good one.

***

I find him at my desk and go to him worried. I set down the bowl of mashed bananas.

"Peter," I whisper.

Nothing.

"Peter," I try again, this time closer to his ear.

Nothing.

I panic. "Peter!" I yell.

I give him a soft, yet firm, shake with my free hand; he doesn't respond. I drop the glass of water and holler, "Joseph! Joseph!"

He runs into the room, takes in the situation, and calmly helps me move my husband back onto the bed. The whole time I'm whispering to Peter, "It's going to be okay, it's going to be okay," through my tears. We lay him on his back. That's when I notice the calmness that's settled there. No more grimace of pain, no more distress. And I understand: He is no longer with me.

I sit beside him and take his hand. I kiss his lips and whisper his name.

***

After a while, I hear rustling behind me and I feel two hands on my shoulders.

"Come, Liana. Caressa's here. She needs to check him."

I allow Joseph to help me up, and I watch Caressa

enter the room. She touches my arm briefly and goes about the business of recording my husband's death.

Unable to breathe and with a heart loaded with emotion, I walk to the living room. There, Joseph helps make me somewhat comfortable and leaves after saying something to me that I don't register.

There, sitting alone, looking out of my window, I let my tears fall freely. I am unashamed in my grief. The fact that I knew this day was coming doesn't make it any easier. Even if I would've had more time, I wouldn't have been able to prepare.

"Here, Liana," says Joseph, sitting beside me. "I made you some tea."

I nod without turning to look at him, and he sets a cup of fragrant chamomile tea on the table in front of me. I look at the table and see my wedding picture. On impulse, I pick it up and hold it to my chest as I continue to cry. Joseph stays beside me with an arm over my shoulder, crying his own tears. I don't know how long we sit like this.

I think about how happy I was this morning. How I felt so optimistic. How I had convinced myself that today was going to be a good day. I feel so ashamed. How could I have laughed, probably, at the exact moment that my husband died?

Suddenly Joseph pulls my face to his chest and I hear wheels on the floor. They're wheeling my husband out of my house, and Joseph is protecting me from having to see. My tears come from somewhere deep within me, with such force that I'm almost convulsing. He holds me tighter. I can feel his tears falling on my head, and I am thankful to have someone with me who has truly loved Peter. I put my arms around him and hold him as tightly as I possibly can.

Words are unnecessary. There's nothing we could say to make this better. Gradually our tears subside and I pull away from him. I immediately regret doing so.

"Would you like a fresh cup of tea?" he asks hoarsely.

I look at the cup which I haven't yet touched, and nod.

While he's gone, I begin thinking about how I found my husband—at my desk—and I wonder what he was doing. It must have been important for him to not wait for help. On heavy feet, I stand and head for the bedroom.

Once there, I avoid looking at the bed, which is still burdened with the messiness of death. I go to the desk and find what my husband was doing.

One sheet of paper, a few words. With a crushing force, I realize what my husband has been doing during the last few months of his life. I comprehend the gift he has given me and realize the depth of his love. I fall to my knees.

***

Joseph comes into the room. I look at him, hold up the sheet of paper, and with tears streaming down my face say, "It was him. This whole time, the letters were from him."

EPILOGUE

Two years have passed since I buried Peter. His last wishes were written in a letter he had left with Joseph. We had a service with his favorite music playing in the background, and when it was time to lower the casket, we did so to the lyrics of "Goodbye" by Air Supply. The sun had glowed bright, birds had fluttered in the sky, the clouds had been fluffy and light. The day had been beautiful, accepting him in its fold.

I still go back and read Peter's letters on occasion. I'm thankful for the gift he gave me. It reinforced the love that I felt for him and still do.

At a time when I had felt lost, Peter gave me something to look forward to. Letters that allowed me to carry on. And without knowing it he gave me the biggest gift of all: hope.

Hope for a better tomorrow. For a different kind of love.

***

I awaken to find an envelope on the pillow beside me underneath a pink lotus flower. I smile, pick the two up, and close my eyes as I smell the flower. I hold the envelope against me for a beat. Then I open it and untuck the single sheet of paper it holds.

Hello beautiful.

That's all it says. That's all I need.

I hear movement at the door and turn to find Joseph, now my husband, standing there holding a small flower arrangement and wearing only a pair of shorts. I smile as he walks to me.

I sit up and the bedsheet falls away from me. We haven't been married long, and we're still learning each other. I reach for the sheet.

"Don't," he says, sitting on the bed, watching me. "You are the most beautiful, wonderful, amazingly strong woman I know. And I love seeing you like this," he says as he caresses my breast with a flower's petals.

I feel so incredibly wonderful. I reach for him and pull him to me. I kiss him over and over until I am utterly satisfied. His skin on mine is pure ecstasy, ethereal bliss. He lies beside me, one hand propping up his head and the other holding onto my behind. There is not a single part of us that isn't touching and he says, looking into my eyes all the way to my core, "You are the best thing that's ever happened to me. You are my heart and soul and my reason for being. I love you."

Tears escape me—I hear what I've always wanted to hear—and I roll him onto his back.